NOT SO FAST

"The *Rockport* doesn't leave until tomorrow," Fargo said. "Stay in your room at the boardinghouse tonight, just to make sure you don't run into Mullaney. Can you manage that, Cord?"

"Of course I can," the young man replied, frowning in indignation. "Do you think I can't control myself for one night?"

"I'll keep an eye on him," Laurie promised.

The door into the restaurant opened, and Denny said, "We don't have to worry about running into Mr. Mullaney. He's here now."

Fargo looked up and saw a murderous scowl on the face of Owen Mullaney as the man glared at them over the twin muzzles of a double-barreled shotgun. . . .

THE
TRAILSMAN
#335

RIVERBOAT RAMPAGE

by

Jon Sharpe

A SIGNET BOOK

SIGNET
Published by New American Library, a division of
Penguin Group (USA) Inc., 375 Hudson Street,
New York, New York 10014, USA
Penguin Group (Canada), 90 Eglinton Avenue East, Suite 700, Toronto,
Ontario M4P 2Y3, Canada (a division of Pearson Penguin Canada Inc.)
Penguin Books Ltd., 80 Strand, London WC2R 0RL, England
Penguin Ireland, 25 St. Stephen's Green, Dublin 2,
Ireland (a division of Penguin Books Ltd.)
Penguin Group (Australia), 250 Camberwell Road, Camberwell, Victoria 3124,
Australia (a division of Pearson Australia Group Pty. Ltd.)
Penguin Books India Pvt. Ltd., 11 Community Centre, Panchsheel Park,
New Delhi - 110 017, India
Penguin Group (NZ), 67 Apollo Drive, Rosedale, North Shore 0632,
New Zealand (a division of Pearson New Zealand Ltd.)
Penguin Books (South Africa) (Pty.) Ltd., 24 Sturdee Avenue,
Rosebank, Johannesburg 2196, South Africa

Penguin Books Ltd., Registered Offices:
80 Strand, London WC2R 0RL, England

First published by Signet, an imprint of New American Library,
a division of Penguin Group (USA) Inc.

First Printing, September 2009
10 9 8 7 6 5 4 3 2 1

The first chapter of this book previously appeared in *Colorado Clash*, the three hundred
thirty-fourth volume in this series.

Copyright © Penguin Group (USA) Inc., 2009
All rights reserved

 REGISTERED TRADEMARK—MARCA REGISTRADA

Printed in the United States of America

The Trailsman

Beginnings . . . they bend the tree and they mark the man. Skye Fargo was born when he was eighteen. Terror was his midwife, vengeance his first cry. Killing spawned Skye Fargo, ruthless, cold-blooded murder. Out of the acrid smoke of gunpowder still hanging in the air, he rose, cried out a promise never forgotten.

The Trailsman they began to call him all across the West: searcher, scout, hunter, the man who could see where others only looked, his skills for hire but not his soul, the man who lived each day to the fullest, yet trailed each tomorrow. Skye Fargo, the Trailsman, the seeker who could take the wildness of a land and the wanting of a woman and make them his own.

The Missouri River, 1860—the Big Muddy will run red with blood when Skye Fargo rides a riverboat to Hell.

1

Raucous shouting attracted the attention of the big man in buckskins. He looked toward the docks and saw a large group of people gathered around something, blocking his sight of whatever it was. Skye Fargo gave a mental shrug and pointed the big, black-and-white Ovaro stallion toward his destination, a waterfront tavern called Red Mike's.

Then somebody in the crowd behind him let out a whoop and yelled, "Kill him, Owen! Bash the dummy's brains out!"

That prompted a burst of laughter, and somebody else shouted, "He can't do that! The dummy ain't got no brains!"

Fargo reined the Ovaro to a halt. His mouth quirked at the irony.

Then he turned the stallion around and headed back toward the commotion at the docks.

With his buckskins, close-cropped dark beard, and broad-brimmed hat, Fargo looked like the veteran frontiersman he was. A long-barreled Colt .44 rode in a holster at his hip, and tucked into a sheath strapped to his right calf was a heavy-bladed Arkansas Toothpick. The butt of a Henry repeater stuck up from a saddle boot. Plenty of men out here went armed. With Skye Fargo, it was like the weapons were part of his body.

He reined in again. Now that he was closer, he could

see over the heads of the crowd. The shouting men formed a circle around a couple of hombres who were fighting.

Or rather, one of the men was fighting. The other had his thick, muscular arms raised and his head hunched down as far as it would go between his massive shoulders. He just stood there, absorbing the punishment that his opponent dealt out. The look on his face was one of dull confusion, as if he couldn't understand why the other man was hitting him.

The man doing the punching was big, too, and dressed like one of the dockworkers. He had a thatch of dark hair and a mustache that curled up on the ends. The sleeves of his shirt were rolled up over brawny forearms. The ham-like fists at the ends of those arms shot out again and again, thudding into the body of the younger man.

The spectators kept up their whooping and hollering as they made bets on the outcome. Fargo watched and saw that most of the action seemed to be going through a slender young man who stood to one side, a bowler hat pushed back on his curly, light brown hair. Fargo's lake blue eyes narrowed as his gaze went back and forth between that young man and the one the dockworker was thrashing.

Fargo thought he saw a family resemblance between the two youngsters. Unless he missed his guess, they were brothers.

The massacre—you couldn't really call it a fight—continued for long minutes. The dockworker's fists had opened up several cuts around his opponent's eyes. Blood smeared the young man's face.

One of the spectators cupped his hands around his mouth and yelled, "Finish him off, Owen! This is gettin' boring!"

Grinning, Owen cocked his fists and angled in, poised for the knockout.

The youngster in the bowler hat reached up and tugged on the brim.

The young man who'd been getting pounded finally threw a punch, a slow, ponderous roundhouse right. At least, the blow appeared slow and ponderous at first. But somehow it made its way past Owen's suddenly frantic attempt to block it and exploded on the dockworker's jaw. A collective "Oh!" of shock came from the crowd as Owen went up in the air, his feet rising several inches off the ground before he came crashing back down on the ground. He twitched a couple of times and then lay still, with his eyes rolled back in their sockets.

Silence reigned over the crowd now.

The youngster in the bowler hat rushed over to his brother. "Are you all right, Denny?" he asked anxiously. "Did he hurt you?"

"Nuh . . . no, I reckon I'm all right, Cord," Denny said. "Did I hurt that fella? I didn't mean to hurt him. I just wanted him to stop whalin' on me."

Tears began to run from Denny's eyes and down his moon face.

"I didn't mean to hurt him!" he wailed.

One of the spectators stepped forward and said, "Uh, that's all right, young fella. Don't worry about it. Owen's kind of a mean son of a bitch anyway. He's the one who picked a fight with you."

Denny kept blubbering. Cord reached around his shoulders, or tried to, anyway, and started to lead him away. The crowd parted to let them through.

"It's all right, it's all right," Cord murmured to his brother. "Everybody knows you didn't mean to hurt anybody, Denny."

That just made Denny cry harder. Cord patted him on the back, which was as wide and sturdy as a stone wall.

"Hey, young fella!" one of the spectators called. "You forgot about your money."

Cord looked back, evidently confused. "Money? Oh!" His expression cleared. "The bets."

"Yeah." The man stepped forward and crammed some greenbacks in Cord's hand. "I don't welsh on my bets. That brother o' yours got damned lucky when he landed that punch, but that don't matter. He still won, so I'm payin' off."

"Me, too," another man said. One by one, all the members of the crowd who had bet against Denny gathered around Cord and handed money to him.

"I feel bad about taking this," Cord protested. "Like that fella said: Denny just got lucky. I never dreamed he'd win. The only reason I backed him was family pride, you know. A man can't bet against his own brother."

"No, sir, he sure can't," one of the men agreed. "You should take that brother of yours and get him a good meal. Maybe some licorice candy. That'll make him feel better."

"You know, I think it just might," Cord said. "Thank you."

One of the spectators nudged another and said, "Let's drag Owen over to the water trough and dunk his head. That ought to wake him up."

"Yeah," agreed the other man. He turned to Cord and Denny. "Mister, you and your brother best get on out of here. Owen ain't gonna be happy when he wakes up. He can be a real son of a bitch when he's mad."

"Just like an old grizzly bear," another man said.

Cord nodded. "Thanks. We'll do that. Come on, Denny."

He led Denny down the street, away from the docks. Still seated on the Ovaro at the edge of the crowd, Fargo watched them go.

Then, after a moment, he walked the stallion after them.

Cord and Denny turned a corner, and as soon as they were out of sight of the docks, Cord tugged on his brother's sleeve and started moving faster. Fargo trailed them until they reached a run-down saloon several blocks from the waterfront. They went inside.

Fargo started to turn and ride away, but his curiosity got the better of him. He swung down from the saddle, looped the Ovaro's reins around the hitch rail in front of the saloon, and followed the two youngsters inside.

The saloon was a narrow, dingy room with a bar along the right side and a scattering of scarred, wobbly tables. Cord and Denny were alone at the end of the bar. Cord already had a drink in his hand. He tossed it back while Denny stood beside him, wiping away blood as it trickled from the cuts around his eyes.

Fargo ambled along the bar and stopped not far from the brothers. When a bullet-headed bartender in a dirty apron came over and raised bushy eyebrows in a questioning look, Fargo said, "Whiskey."

The drink juggler splashed amber liquid from an unlabeled bottle into a glass that wasn't too smeared with fingerprints. Fargo expected the whiskey to be bad, and it was. Just one step above panther piss, in fact. But he sipped it anyway and said, "Pretty slick."

Cord's eyes cut over toward him. "You talking to me, mister?"

"That's right," Fargo replied. "I said that was pretty slick, what you and your brother just pulled."

"I don't know what you're talking about," Cord said

with a quick shake of his head. He shoved his empty glass back across the bar. "Come on, Denny."

Fargo turned to block their path. "Hold on. I'm not looking for trouble, son."

"Then don't start any," Cord warned.

"I'm just curious, that's all," Fargo went on as if he hadn't heard what Cord said.

"Curious about what?"

"How many times the two of you have pulled that little game."

Cord shook his head. "I still don't know what you're talking about, and if you don't get out of the way, Denny will *put* you out of the way."

It was Fargo's turn to issue a warning. "You might not want to do that," he said. "You see, unlike his last opponent—or should I say victim—I know how fast and how strong Denny is. He won't take me by surprise."

Cord was starting to look worried now. "Mister, what the hell is it you want?"

Fargo wasn't quite sure of the answer to that question. He had ridden into Saint Louis to pick up some supplies before starting west again, but he'd decided to detour by Red Mike's because he had good memories of a gal who worked there. At least, she had a year or two earlier. She might have moved on by now.

Then he had seen and heard the commotion at the docks and had decided to take a look. That had led him here.

"Why don't I buy the two of you a good meal?" he suggested. "You look like you could use it."

Cord sneered. "We've got our own money. We don't need any handouts."

"Yeah, that's right. You've got the money you won from the bets placed on your brother. Do you share that with him, or do you keep it all for yourself?"

Fargo had decided he didn't like Cord. It looked to him like the youngster was taking advantage of his brother. Denny's slow-witted ways weren't a pose, even though he was a much more dangerous fighter than he had appeared to be at first as he allowed the dockworker called Owen to land punch after punch.

Cord's face flushed with anger at Fargo's question. "I'm tired of this," he snapped. "Denny, teach this son of a bitch a lesson."

Denny stepped away from the bar and bunched his fists, but he hesitated. "You sure, Cord? I don't think he's as dumb as that other fella was."

"You let me worry about who's dumb and who's not, damn it! Just do what I told you!"

Denny looked at Fargo, shook his head, and shrugged. "Sorry, mister," he said.

Then with blinding speed he stepped past his brother and shot a looping punch at Fargo.

The blow would have taken Fargo's head off if it had connected. Instead, Fargo weaved away from it with some speed of his own. Denny's big fist whipped harmlessly past his ear.

The missed punch threw Denny off balance. Fargo stepped closer, grabbed the massive youngster's arm, and twisted it up behind Denny's back. Denny was strong, but so was Fargo, and now Fargo had the advantage. He could have broken the arm, but instead he put just enough pressure on it to make Denny howl in pain.

"Hey!" the bartender yelled. "You bust up the place, you'll pay for it, both of you!"

"Cord!" Denny cried. "Cord, he's hurtin' me! Make him stop!"

Pale-faced now, Cord reached behind his back and came out with a small pistol that must have been tucked in his belt, under his shirt.

"Let him go, mister!" he yelled at Fargo. "Let him go, or I swear I'll shoot!"

On the other side of the hardwood, the bartender ducked behind the bar, getting out of the way in case bullets started to fly. The handful of customers in the saloon, who had been watching the confrontation with idle, boozed-up interest, abandoned their tables and scurried for the door.

"Put that popgun away," Fargo snapped. "As big as your brother is, you're a lot more liable to hit him than me. And if he'll stop struggling, it won't hurt near as bad."

Cord appeared to be torn about what to do next. After a moment, though, he lowered the pistol and said, "Denny, stop it. Quit fighting."

"But he won't let me go!" Denny wailed.

"Just settle down!"

Denny looked shocked that Cord would yell at him. He stopped struggling in Fargo's grip. Fargo eased off a little more.

"I'll let go of him if both of you will promise not to do anything else stupid."

"We don't know you, mister," Cord said. "Trusting you really would be stupid."

The young man had a point, Fargo supposed. He released Denny's arm and stepped back. His hand dropped to the butt of the .44, just in case Cord tried to use that little pistol.

Cord didn't raise the gun again, although he didn't put it away. He said to his brother, "Denny, are you all right?"

Denny was rubbing his sore arm. "Yeah," he said. "You don't still want me to fight that fella, do you, Cord? 'Cause I don't want to."

"No, you don't have to fight him." Awkwardly, Cord

patted Denny on the shoulder. "I shouldn't have gotten you into this mess."

That made Fargo like him a little more. Or dislike him a little less, anyway.

Cord glared at Fargo. "For what it's worth, mister—and it's none of your damned business—Denny always gets his share of whatever we make. I wouldn't cheat my own brother."

"You'd just take advantage of him by making him fight," Fargo shot back.

"I don't mind," Denny said. "Most of the time, it ain't that bad. I'm used to gettin' hit."

"Are you the law?" Cord asked.

Fargo shook his head. "Nope."

"Then you've got no right to interfere with us. We're leaving, and you can't stop us."

Fargo thought he had already demonstrated that he *could* stop them—but Cord was correct. He didn't have any right to do so. And he wasn't in the habit of sticking his nose in other folks' business. This was just a momentary aberration, indulging his curiosity on a whim when he should have known better.

"All right," he said. "Sorry I bothered you. I still say that was pretty slick, though, the way you signaled to your brother by tugging on your hat. That's how he knew when to stop taking the punishment and throw a punch of his own."

Denny stopped rubbing his arm and looked surprised. "Hey, how'd he figure that out, Cord? Nobody else ever has."

"I don't know," Cord said. "Come on, let's go."

"And the crying was a nice touch, too," Fargo went on as they started around him. "It made everybody in the crowd feel sorry for Denny, instead of thinking about how the two of you might have tricked them. If they had tumbled to what was really going on, you might have been in a lot of trouble." He added to their backs, "Something like that, they would have broken out the tar and feathers."

Cord glanced back over his shoulder at Fargo, then shoved Denny on through the batwings at the saloon's entrance.

The bartender had stood up behind the bar when it became obvious there wasn't going to be any shooting. "Are those two young fellas really some sort of flimflam artists, mister?"

Fargo nodded. "That's the way it looked to me."

"Who'd they trick into fightin' the big one?"

"Some hombre called Owen," Fargo said. "Looked like a dockworker."

The bartender's bushy eyebrows rose again, in surprise this time, rather than asking a question. "Not Owen Mullaney? Big bruiser, has a mustache that curls up on the ends?"

"That's him."

The bartender let out a whistle. "Those boys better hope Mullaney doesn't track them down. The law's never been able to prove it, but he's killed three or four men, and he won't like it that he got fooled."

"You think he might go after them?" Fargo asked with a frown.

"You didn't hear it from me . . . but he might. If I was those two young fellas, I reckon I'd get out of town while the gettin' is good."

Cord and Denny didn't know that, though. To them, Owen Mullaney was just another victim of their trickery.

Fargo dropped a coin on the hardwood to pay for the Who-hit-John he had barely touched, then went to the door. He thrust the batwings aside and stepped out, looking both directions along the street as he did so. He wanted to catch up to Cord and Denny and warn them about Mullaney.

But the two young men were nowhere in sight. They were already gone.

Since there was nothing he could do—and it was none of his business, anyway, he reminded himself again—Fargo got on the Ovaro and rode back to the riverfront.

He stopped at Red Mike's as he had planned originally, but the proprietor told him that Bess Dugan no longer worked there. She had moved on some six months earlier, and the man didn't know where.

"These whores, they come and go," he said with a shrug, then laughed at his unintentional joke.

Disappointed, Fargo left the tavern. There was nothing holding him in Saint Louis now, so he could go ahead and pick up his supplies and a packhorse. It was fairly late in the day, however, so he decided he might as well spend one more night under a roof before heading out. He led the Ovaro toward a hotel where he had stayed before.

Saint Louis was the busiest port on the Mississippi River north of New Orleans. It got not only all the traffic from downriver, but the confluence of the Mississippi and the Missouri rivers was only a short distance above the town, so all the riverboats that plied the Missouri departed from Saint Louis as well. Since the Big Muddy, as the Missouri River was sometimes known, was the major route to the northern Rockies and had been ever since Lewis and Clark had followed it almost fifty years earlier, that meant plenty of stern-wheelers churned through its waters.

Because of the heavy river traffic from both north and

south, the docks at Saint Louis were always crowded, and so were the streets. Holding the Ovaro's reins, Fargo weaved among pedestrians, wagons, buggies, and riders on horseback. He also had to avoid the mud puddles and numerous piles of horse and mule droppings. It made for an interesting walk.

Even with those distractions, some instinct made him glance across the street. Maybe he heard a familiar voice. He didn't know.

But he recognized Denny's huge, hulking form right away and then spotted Cord's bowler hat as the other young man hurried along beside his brother.

That was a stroke of luck. Fargo angled toward them, intending to pass along the bartender's warning about Owen Mullaney. Before he could reach them, however, they stopped to talk to a woman they had just encountered, and Fargo paused to study her.

She was worth studying. Tall and slender, but with ample curves on display in the simple woolen dress she wore, she had a mass of red hair that tumbled around her shoulders. Like Cord and Denny, she was young, no more than twenty or so. As Fargo looked at the three of them, he realized suddenly that the woman shared the same family resemblance as the two young men. She had to be their sister.

What happened next seemed to support that hunch. Cord took some money from his pocket and pressed it into the woman's hand. She nodded, then gave him and Denny each a quick hug. It looked like Cord was sharing their winnings with her.

She turned and went into the building they'd been standing in front of, which happened to be a hotel. Cord and Denny started on down the street. Fargo went after them.

He wasn't the only one with instincts. Something must have warned Cord, because he glanced over his shoulder, spotted Fargo, and grabbed Denny's arm. Cord said something to his brother, and then both of them started walking faster.

Fargo increased his own pace, but damned if he was going to run after them. For one thing, the street was too crowded for that. For another, if Cord and Denny had been pulling that same trick for very long, they had probably had some angry hombres coming after them before now. They had to know how to handle trouble on their own, and if they weren't expecting it, that was their own lookout.

The thought of that redheaded gal crying over her brothers if anything happened to them was what prompted Fargo to keep trailing Cord and Denny. Also, it was entirely possible that she'd be left on her own if they were gone, and Fargo knew what a rough time a girl like that would face out here if she were alone.

Up ahead, Cord and Denny ducked into an alley. Fargo hurried after them, but a group of boisterous crew members from one of the docked riverboats suddenly spilled out of a saloon in front of him, blocking his path. They were all drunk and stumbling around, and Fargo had a hard time getting past them. By the time he did, he had a bad feeling about what he would find when his long-legged strides carried him to the alley.

Sure enough, Cord and Denny were gone again. They had vanished like they'd never been there, and Fargo knew that searching for them in the rat's warren of alleys would be a waste of time.

He blew out a frustrated breath and turned around. He knew where the redhead had gone. Maybe he could catch up to her and tell her what the bartender had said about

Owen Mullaney. Surely she would be seeing her brothers again before too long, and she could warn them.

When Fargo got back to the hotel, he tied the Ovaro in front and went in. A glance around the lobby told him the girl wasn't there. He approached the desk.

This was a nice hotel, and fairly expensive. The slick-haired desk clerk wore a dark suit and a cravat with a stickpin in it. He frowned as Fargo came up to the desk.

"May I help you, sir?" he asked, his tone indicating that he thought that was unlikely. In buckskins covered with trail dust, Fargo didn't look anything like this place's usual clientele.

"I'm looking for a woman with red hair," Fargo said. He held out a hand. "About yay tall, nice-looking, around twenty years old. She was wearing a gray wool dress, and I think she might be staying here."

The clerk didn't hesitate. He shook his head and said, "None of our guests match that description, sir. I suggest you try some of the, ah, establishments closer to the river-front."

"She's not a whore or a saloon gal," Fargo snapped, feeling a surge of annoyance at this prig's attitude. Even as he made that declaration, though, he realized that he couldn't be sure he was right about her. She might be either of those things.

"There's still nothing I can do to help you," the clerk insisted. "The only person in the hotel who looks like the woman you described is that girl."

He pointed. Fargo turned to look and saw a young woman with a maid's cap on her red hair, carrying what appeared to be a load of clean bedding toward the stairs.

She was the same woman he had seen talking to Cord and Denny.

"That's her," Fargo said. He took a step toward her and called, "Miss! Wait a minute, miss. I need to talk to you."

14

At the foot of the stairs, she turned, gasped, dropped the bedding, and reached into the pocket of her dress. She came up with a knife and brandished it at Fargo as she said, "Don't come another step closer! I'll cut you if you do!"

2

"Oh, dear Lord!" the clerk exclaimed behind Fargo. "You can't go around threatening people like that. Put that knife away, girl, right now!"

The redhead glanced past Fargo and snapped, "Shut up, or I'll carve you, too, you fancy-dressed little pipsqueak!"

While she was looking away, Fargo took a fast step forward. That brought him within reach. The redhead cried out and tried to stab him, but he was too fast for her. His left hand closed around her wrist and pushed it to the side so that the blade didn't come anywhere close to him. A quick twist made her release the knife. As it fell to the floor, luckily missing their feet, Fargo looped his other arm around her and jerked her toward him.

"Settle down," he told her. "Nobody's going to hurt you."

"You're already hurting me, you bastard! Let me go!"

Fargo slid his left hand up her right arm and got hold of her left arm with his right hand. With both arms immobilized, she kicked at him instead. Fargo twirled her around, pulled her arms behind her, and captured her wrists in one big hand, holding them with his left while he clamped his right on her shoulder and said, "Stop fighting. There's no need for this."

The desk clerk said, "Should I summon the authorities?"

"No!" Fargo and the redhead said together. As she glanced back at him in surprise, he went on, "See? That proves we're on the same side."

"What do you want with me, mister? I never even saw you before."

"Then why'd you pull a knife on me?" Fargo asked. "You must have some idea who I am, even if it's wrong." Understanding dawned on him. "Your brothers described me to you, didn't they?"

"Cord said you were after him and Denny for some reason, and that I ought to watch out for you. He said you were a big bastard in buckskins."

The clerk said, "Could . . . could the two of you possibly take this discussion somewhere else?"

Without loosening his grip on the redhead, Fargo glanced around. Quite a few people were in the hotel lobby, and they were all staring at him and the girl.

"I reckon we must be bad for business," he said dryly. "Let's go out back. I've got something important to tell you. And I'll let you go if you promise not to run off or try to stab me again."

"I can't stab you. I dropped my knife." She hesitated. "But I promise, if that'll get you to let me go."

Fargo released her wrists, but he kept the hand on her shoulder until he had bent over and plucked the knife from the floor. Then he took his hand off her shoulder as well and stepped back, tucking the knife behind his belt. The redhead looked back at him, shrugged, and then started along the corridor that ran behind the stairs, toward the rear of the hotel.

"You're dismissed from employment, by the way!" the clerk called after her.

She gave Fargo an accusing look. "See what you did?"

"I just wanted to talk to you," he said. "You're the one who started waving a knife around for no reason."

17

"I had a good reason. My brothers warned me about you."

Fargo just shook his head. He didn't know if she was going to listen to reason. Maybe she would once he told her about Owen Mullaney.

She opened the rear door, and they stepped out into the alley behind the hotel. The air stunk of garbage back here. To tell the truth, the air stunk just about everywhere in Saint Louis, as far as Fargo was concerned. He was used to the clean, clear atmosphere of the high country. To a certain extent, almost every settlement smelled bad to him.

He closed the door behind them and said, "What's your name?"

She just gave him a sullen look, and for a moment he thought she wasn't going to answer. Then she shrugged and said, "Laurie."

"Laurie what?"

"Trahearne."

"Well, listen to me, Laurie Trahearne," Fargo said. "Someone may be looking for your brothers and intending to do them harm, but it's not me. It's a man named Owen Mullaney."

He could tell from the genuinely puzzled look she gave him that she'd never heard of Mullaney before. "Who's that?" she asked.

"The dockworker Denny got in that phony fight with earlier this afternoon."

"There was nothing phony about it!" Laurie protested. "Denny really got hit. I know it hurt him."

"I'm sure it did," Fargo agreed, "but he could have ended the fight anytime he wanted to. He waited, though, until Cord gave him the signal."

Fargo reached up and tugged on the brim of his Stetson, just to show her that he knew what he was talking about.

Laurie crossed her arms over her breasts and glared at him. "That doesn't mean the fight was phony."

"They've got the act down pretty well," Fargo said. "How does it work? Denny pretends to bump into somebody who's likely to take offense and prod him into a fight? I'll bet Cord even pretends to try to talk the hombre out of it, but all the while he's really egging him on. Then a crowd gathers, and the first punch is thrown, and men being men, they start to bet . . ."

"All right!" Laurie said. "All right, you figured it all out. What do you want from me?"

"The next time you see your brothers, tell them that they picked the wrong man this time. He's dangerous. According to what I've been told, Mullaney has killed several men. He won't like being knocked out like he was, in front of a bunch of his friends, and once he figures out that Cord and Denny set him up, he's going to be even angrier. He might come after them and try to settle the score. They need to get out of Saint Louis, and if they can't do that, they ought to at least lie low for a while."

Laurie's peaches-and-cream complexion had paled even more while Fargo was talking. When he finished, she said, "Is that true? Are they really in danger?"

"If what I was told is accurate, then yes, they are."

"Oh, Lord." Laurie closed her eyes and put a hand to her temple for a second. "I warned them. . . . I told them they were going to push things too far one of these days. . . . I have this job here at the hotel. I told them to just be patient." She looked up at Fargo. "I should say, I *had* this job at the hotel. Now that's gone."

"I'll talk to the clerk if you'd like," Fargo offered. "Maybe I can convince him to give you your job back."

"I doubt it. That prissy little weasel's got more back-bone than you'd think to look at him. The other day he even put his hand on my—well, never mind." She shook her head. "I'll find Cord and Denny and warn them." Grudgingly, she added, "Thanks, I guess."

"Do you think they'll leave town?"

"We were all going to, as soon as we saved up enough money to buy our passage on one of the riverboats head-ing up the Missouri. Another week or so would have done it." She frowned in thought. "Maybe we have enough for the two of them to go on ahead without me. I can always come later."

"What about Mullaney?"

"He doesn't know who *I* am. I won't be in any danger from him."

She was probably right about that, Fargo thought. But even so, a lovely young woman on her own was always going to be in some danger in a place like this. It would be better if Laurie could head upriver with her brothers, as they had planned.

"Listen," he said, "I've got a little money—"

"Forget it," she said. "I don't take money from strange men. You know what that would make me."

"Well, then, don't consider me a stranger." He put out a hand. "My name is Skye Fargo."

She hesitated, then took his hand. "That's an unusual name. But it suits you."

"Why don't I come with you while you find your brothers?" Fargo suggested. "You can pool your money and see how much you need for all three of you to be able to leave Saint Louis. If you're close to having enough, I'll make up the difference."

"Why would you do that? Out of the kindness of your heart?"

"Some people *are* kind from time to time, you know."

She snorted derisively. "If that's true, I've never seen it. People have always treated us like dirt. We've had to make our own way in the world ever since our ma died a few years ago."

"Where's your father?"

Laurie gestured vaguely toward the northwest. "Out there somewhere on the frontier. The last time we heard from him, he was at Fort Benton. That's why we're going up the Missouri, to see if we can find him. But that was five years ago, so there's no telling where he is now, or even if he's still alive."

"What's his name?" Fargo asked. "I've been to Fort Benton a few times. I might've run into him."

A faint flicker of hope appeared in her eyes. "Isaac Trahearne," she said.

Fargo thought about it for a moment, then shook his head. "Sorry. Can't say as the name means anything to me." As he saw the disappointment on her face, he added, "But that doesn't mean he's not there. Fort Benton's grown quite a bit. I don't know everybody who lives there."

"Well, we can hope, anyway, I guess. And if you're sure you want to help us . . ."

"I do," Fargo said.

"Let's go see if we can find them, then. I know most of the places where they spend their time."

Fargo reached behind him and took the knife from his belt. He held it out to her. "I reckon I can trust you with this now? You won't try to stab me again?"

"We'll see," she said.

Laurie didn't want to go back through the hotel. She took off the maid's cap and threw it on the ground, muttering, "Good riddance." Then she and Fargo went around the building and back out onto the street.

"Where have you been staying?" Fargo asked.

"We've got a room in a boardinghouse. It's the cheapest place we could find. Denny hung up a blanket so I can have a little privacy."

"Where are you from?"

She looked sideways at him. "You sure do ask a lot of questions, mister."

"Call me Skye," he suggested.

"I reckon I'll call you Mr. Fargo, if I call you anything," she said. "As for where we're from, we grew up on a farm in Ohio. Then Pa decided to come west to make his fortune and left us there. We lost the farm for taxes after a bad year, and we had to move in with some relatives in Cincinnati. It wasn't too bad for a while, but after Ma passed on, my uncle started getting a mite too fresh with me. Cord said we had to get out, either that or kill the old goat, so we left. We made it on whatever odd jobs we could get, until Cord came up with the idea of . . ."

"Of using Denny to make money in those fights," Fargo finished for her when her words trailed away.

Laurie's face flushed. "I don't like it. But folks have to do things they don't like all the time, if they want to get by."

That was true, Fargo thought. Most people didn't have the luxury he did, of being able to go wherever the wild wind took them.

Laurie led him to several saloons and hash houses frequented by her brothers. They didn't find Cord and Denny at any of the places. Fargo could tell that Laurie's frustration was growing, along with her worry.

"Do you think Mullaney might have found them already?" she asked. "Oh, God, what if he's killed them?"

"I'll see to it that the law deals with him," Fargo promised, knowing even as he spoke them that the words would sound pretty hollow to her.

"The law," she said bitterly. "The law doesn't give a damn about people like us who don't have any money."

Fargo knew that all too often, that was true. "Then *I'll* deal with Mullaney," he said.

"Why? Just because it's the right thing to do?"

"Well . . . yeah." Fargo paused. "You don't have much faith in human nature, do you?"

"Sure I do. I have faith it's all bad." She put her hands on her hips and looked around. "I can think of one other place they might be. I don't particularly want to go there, but I don't see any way around it."

"Tell me where it is, and I'll go by myself," Fargo said.

"That won't work. If Cord and Denny see you without me, they'll just take off running again. They don't trust you."

"That's a good point," Fargo admitted. "Lead on."

Laurie sighed. "It's this way. . . ."

Several blocks later, Fargo realized where they were going before they got there. He'd never patronized the place himself, but he had heard about it.

"Are you headed for Jenny's?" he asked.

She gave him a caustic look. "I should have figured you'd know about it. You being a man and all, I mean."

"I've never set foot in the place," Fargo said.

"Hmmph." The snort clearly expressed her disbelief.

From the outside, the place was a ramshackle old stone mansion. Weeds grew around the wrought-iron fence and through the cracks in the flagstone walk that led to the front porch. The men who patronized the establishment didn't care about the outside, only what they could buy inside.

The gate opened with a squeal of rusty hinges as Laurie pushed on it. "I'll shoot myself before I wind up in a place like this," she muttered as she and Fargo started up the walk.

When they reached the porch, Fargo used a fist to knock on the door. It swung open after a moment, and the woman who stood there in a silk wrapper smiled at Fargo. The expression was automatic, but it held some genuine admiration as she ran her eyes over his muscular frame. She still possessed some faded beauty. Dark hair piled on her head was only lightly touched with gray. In a voice that held the rasp of too many late nights and too much whiskey and laudanum, she said, "Hello, honey. Welcome to—" The woman stopped short as she noticed Laurie standing there with Fargo. "You again," she said coldly.

"I'm looking for my brothers, Miss Jenny."

"Who're you?" the madam asked Fargo. "Not another brother, I hope?"

"Nope." Fargo inclined his head toward Laurie. "But I *am* with Miss Trahearne here."

"Wouldn't want to make some money, would you, handsome? Talk her into working for me, and I'll give you a cut for the first month. Some of my customers really like redheads. Can't have too many of 'em in this business."

"We're just looking for Cord and Denny," Laurie said. "Are they here?"

"Yeah, yeah," the madam said with a weary nod as she moved back. "The big one's sitting in the parlor, like always. The other one's upstairs."

Fargo and Laurie walked into the house. Even though it was afternoon outside, thick curtains over all the windows ensured a state of perpetual twilight within. The red-shaded lamps did little to dispel the gloom. As far as Fargo could tell, the house was fairly well furnished.

As they went into the parlor, Fargo spotted Denny sitting on a brocaded sofa, flanked by a couple of half-naked women who leaned against his massive form, laughing and talking suggestively to him. Even in the bad light, Fargo could tell that Denny's face was bright red.

Denny bolted to his feet as he saw Fargo, almost spilling the soiled doves who'd been tormenting him onto the floor. "You again!" he cried. "Cord said—"

Laurie stepped up beside Fargo and said, "Forget about what Cord said, Denny. This is Mr. Fargo. He doesn't want to hurt you, or any of us."

"Laurie! But"—Denny looked back and forth between Fargo and Laurie, clearly confused—"Cord said—"

"I told you, forget about what Cord said. Mr. Fargo is . . . a friend."

Fargo heard the slight hesitation. Denny didn't seem to notice it, though. He stared at Fargo and repeated, "A friend?"

"That's right," Fargo said. "I want to help you and Cord get out of Saint Louis."

A hopeful look appeared on Denny's face. "So we can find our pa?"

"That's right."

"Well, then, somebody should go get Cord, so's we can tell him about it." Denny looked at the ceiling. "He's upstairs. He said he had to go help one of the girls who lives here straighten some things out."

Laurie cleared her throat and said, "Never you mind about that, Denny. I'm sure he'll be down soon."

Fargo tightened his jaw to keep from grinning. Laurie scowled over at him.

"I don't know," Denny said. He lowered his voice to a rumble. "Some o' these girls seem mighty confused about things. You should'a heard some of the things they said to me—"

Laurie held up a hand to stop him. "That's all right, Denny. I'll take your word for it. Right now, why don't we go outside? We can wait for Cord on the porch."

"All right." Again he tried to whisper. "To tell you the truth, I think it smells better outside."

Fargo couldn't argue with that. The scent of cologne was so thick and sickly sweet it was cloying. As they left the parlor, one of the soiled doves called after them, "You come back anytime, Denny. We're always glad to see you, big boy."

In the foyer, Jenny said, "When Cord comes down, I'll tell him you're out there waiting for him."

"Thank you," Laurie said stiffly.

"You know, honey, you really need to do something about that ramrod you got stuck up your—"

Fargo took hold of Laurie's arm, steered her on out the door, and tugged on his hat brim with his other hand as he said, "Ma'am," to Jenny.

"What was Miss Jenny talkin' about, Laurie?" Denny asked as he followed them onto the porch. "You don't have a ramrod. We don't even have a rifle."

"Don't worry about it," she told him. She gestured toward the top step. "Just sit down."

Denny obeyed without question. Fargo and Laurie sat on a bench to the right of the front door.

Keeping his voice low, he said, "The three of you don't have money to buy passage to Fort Benton, but Cord can afford to visit this place?"

"He says a man has needs."

"What a man needs is to have some priorities."

"I'll bet you're a fine one to talk."

"What does that mean?" Fargo asked. "You haven't known me much more than an hour. That's not very long to decide what a fella's like."

Laurie didn't answer. She turned her head away from Fargo. The past few years must have been mighty rough on her, he thought, to make her put up such a wall between herself and everybody else.

And there he was, doing the same thing he had accused her of doing, he told himself with a smile. He was jumping to conclusions just like she was. More of that human nature they had talked about, he supposed.

The strained silence persisted for another ten minutes or so, and then the front door opened and Cord stepped out, a wary look on his face. "You!" he exclaimed as he recognized Fargo. His hand reached behind his back. "When Jenny told me there was somebody out here with Denny and Laurie, I should've known it would be you!"

Fargo uncoiled from the bench. "Leave that gun where it is, Cord," he said. "I'm not looking for trouble."

"Oh, no?" Cord challenged. "Then why the hell have you been following us all afternoon?"

"Because I've got something important to tell you."

"I think you should listen to him, Cord," Laurie said as she stood up, too. "He says he wants to help us, and I believe Mr. Fargo's telling the truth."

"Mr. Fargo?" Cord repeated. "Mighty friendly with him, ain't you, Laurie?" He frowned. "Wait a minute. Skye Fargo?"

"That's right," Fargo said.

"You know him?" Laurie asked with a frown of her own.

Cord didn't answer her. Instead he said to Fargo, "The one they call the Trailsman?"

"Some do," Fargo admitted.

"Cord!"

"Hold on, hold on," Cord told his sister. "I never met

him before today, but I've heard fellas talk about him in saloons. He's supposed to be famous. Guides wagon trains, scouts for the army, fights Indians and outlaws, that sort of thing. Like Kit Carson."

"I know old Kit," Fargo said. "Rode with him a few times. It's been a while, though."

"Why would somebody like the Trailsman want to help a bunch of no-accounts like us?"

Laurie's chin jutted out defiantly. "Speak for yourself, Cord Trahearne!"

"Listen," Fargo said. "Your sister has told me about your problems, and I'd like to do what I can to see that you get out of Saint Louis safely."

"What do you mean by that?"

"That fella Owen Mullaney, the one Denny tangled with a while ago? According to what I've been told, he's a bad man to cross."

Cord snorted and shook his head. "Denny put him down with one punch, just like all the others."

"That's because he took him by surprise. Mullaney won't be fooled again. If he comes looking for you, he'll be ready to dish out some real trouble."

Laurie said, "He's killed men before, Cord. He's liable to try to kill you and Denny."

Cord tried not to show it, but even though he succeeded in keeping a smug look on his face, Fargo saw the near panic that shot through the young man's eyes. "I'm not scared of any big blowhard," Cord insisted, "and I'm not gonna let anybody stampede us into running away."

"We were going to Fort Benton anyway," Laurie argued. "Why can't we just head on upriver now?"

"We don't have enough money, that's why. Give me and Denny another week. Together with the wages from that job of yours at the hotel—"

"I don't have that job anymore," Laurie broke in. "I was dismissed."

"What? How the hell did that happen?"

Fargo said, "You told your sister about me and got her so spooked she pulled a knife on me when I tried to talk to her. I had to take it away from her."

Cord started to reach for his gun again. "You've ruined everything, mister."

"Cord, stop it!" Laurie said. "Fighting with Mr. Fargo isn't going to do any good. I learned that. Anyway, he's on our side. He wants to help us get away from Mullaney." She put a hand on Cord's arm. "He said he'd help pay for our passage to Fort Benton."

Cord sneered. "Yeah? And what does he want in return? Did he tell you that, Laurie?"

As Laurie flushed in embarrassment, Fargo said, "For a young fella, you've sure learned how to be mighty annoying, Cord. I don't want anything in return. But if you don't want my help . . ." He shrugged and started to turn away.

"Wait a minute," Cord said. "Just hang on. I'm trying to figure this out. I ain't used to people helping anybody out of the goodness of their heart."

"Your sister said about the same thing to me."

Laurie's hand tightened on Cord's arm. "Don't be a damned fool. We can at least listen to him."

"And have dinner with me," Fargo suggested. He had enough money for that, too, with enough left over to buy their passage on a riverboat and pick up the supplies he wanted. If he did happen to run short, he could sit in on a poker game for a while and build up his stake without much trouble.

After a moment, Cord nodded. "All right. We'll go eat with you. I still think you're up to something, but I'm willing to listen."

Fargo smiled. "I never saw anybody who was so blasted stubborn about not letting anybody help them."

"Nobody's ever tried to help us before," Laurie said.

They went to a restaurant Fargo knew, where the food was good but not too expensive. There was nothing fancy about it, just a hole-in-the-wall with a few tables covered with blue-checked cloths and a short counter with stools in front of it. A Norwegian couple and their large brood of children ran the place. The stout woman greeted Fargo with a big hug and showed him and the Trahearnes to one of the tables. She yelled into the kitchen, "Papa! Fry up the biggest steak we have, *ja*? Skye Fargo is here!"

"You really are famous, aren't you?" Laurie said to Fargo.

"Maybe 'infamous' would be a better word, depending on how you look at it," he told her.

Over coffee and large platters of food, Fargo listened as they told him more about their lives on the family farm, then in Cincinnati, and finally about the long, hard trek they had made here to Saint Louis. Cord relaxed a little but still seemed wary as he said, "We knew we'd have to make it here before we could even think about going on west to look for our pa. All the riverboats leave from here."

"That's true," Fargo agreed. "There are two or three boats a week heading upriver. As a matter of fact, I think there's one leaving tomorrow. A stern-wheeler called the *Rockport*. The three of you need to be on it."

"Do you think any tickets are still available?" Laurie asked.

"Well, you might have to sleep on the deck," Fargo said. "It may not be pleasant. But it's better than staying here and letting Mullaney try to even the score with Denny and Cord."

"How were we to know he was a vicious lunatic?" Cord demanded.

"People you can trick into trying to thrash somebody like Denny just for the fun of it are liable to be pretty sorry specimens," Fargo pointed out.

"Yeah, maybe."

Denny said, "What do you mean, somebody like me, Mr. Fargo?"

Laurie leaned over to him and said, "He means somebody so big and strong, Denny."

"Oh."

Fargo said, "I'm heading in the direction of Fort Benton myself, but you'll beat me there. If you don't find your father, just stay there until I show up, and I'll help you look for him."

"What if something happens to you along the way?" Cord asked. "You might not ever get there."

"That's a chance we all take," Fargo said. "Use your own judgment."

"Which isn't all that good," Laurie added, "or else you wouldn't have been wasting our money on . . . on trollops."

Denny said, "What are tr-trol . . ."

"The women at Miss Jenny's."

"Oh." Denny's face started to turn red again at the memory.

"The *Rockport* doesn't leave until tomorrow," Fargo said. "Stay in your room at the boardinghouse tonight, just to make sure you don't run into Mullaney. Can you manage that, Cord?"

"Of course I can," the young man replied, frowning in indignation. "Do you think I can't control myself for one night?"

"I'll keep an eye on him," Laurie promised.

The door into the restaurant opened, and Denny said, "We don't have to worry about running into Mr. Mullaney. He's here now."

Fargo looked up and saw a murderous scowl on the face of Owen Mullaney as the man glared at them over the twin muzzles of a double-barreled shotgun.

3

Fargo knew better than to wait for Mullaney to say anything. He exploded up from his chair, taking the table with him. His hands gripped its edges. At the same time, he hooked a foot around a front leg on Laurie's chair and heaved up on it, toppling the chair over backward and sending Laurie out of the line of fire with it.

"Denny, down!" Fargo shouted. He knew Cord would jump for cover without being told.

The muscles in Fargo's arms and shoulders bunched as he rushed toward Mullaney with the thick, heavy table. The shotgun boomed. Fargo felt the impact as the double charge of buckshot slammed into the table. It slowed him a little, but his momentum kept him going and a second later he crashed into Mullaney, ramming him with the table.

Mullaney gave an incoherent shout of rage as he went over backward. Fargo shoved the table aside and kicked the shotgun out of Mullaney's hands. Even though the weapon was empty now, it would still make a pretty good club.

Mullaney was stunned for the moment. Fargo reached down and grabbed the front of the man's shirt. He hauled Mullaney to his feet, drew the Colt, and jammed the revolver's barrel up under the ridge of Mullaney's heavy jaw. His thumb looped over the hammer and drew it back.

The insistent pressure of the gun muzzle brought Mullaney back to his senses. His eyes widened as he must have realized that the slightest pressure on the trigger would blow a big chunk of his head right off.

"Listen to me," Fargo said. "I know you're mad, but it's not worth it. You're not going to come after those kids, Mullaney. You understand me? You're going to leave them alone."

Mullaney swallowed hard. He had to know he was a hairsbreadth away from dying, but his anger was just too much to contain completely.

"They played me for a fool!"

"I know it. It's not worth dying over. And that's what'll happen if you hurt them. I'll kill you."

"Who . . . who the hell are you?"

"Skye Fargo."

Mullaney knew the name. Fargo could tell that by the recognition that flickered in the man's muddy eyes.

"Listen," Fargo said again. "They're leaving Saint Louis. They'll be gone, and everybody will forget about what happened in that fight. You can go on being the big skookum he-wolf around here. Or you can die. The choice is up to you."

Mullaney licked his lips nervously. After a moment he nodded as much as the gun muzzle pressed into his throat would allow. "All right," he said. "As long as they . . . get outta Saint Looie . . . we'll forget about it."

"That's the smart thing to do," Fargo told him. Without looking around, and without taking the gun away from Mullaney's jaw, he said, "Laurie, you and your brothers get out of here. I'll see you later."

"All right, Mr. Fargo," she said. "Cord, Denny, come on."

Fargo heard them leaving the café. He glanced over at the counter and saw the Norwegian couple peeking over the top of it. "Anna, Thor, I'm sorry about the mess and the damage to your table." With his left hand, he reached into a pocket on the buckskin shirt and found a coin. He tossed it in their direction. "This ought to cover it."

"*Ja*, Mr. Fargo, thank you," the husband said as he scurried out from behind the counter, snatched up the coin, then retreated again.

Fargo stepped back but kept the gun pointed at Mullaney. "You're leaving first," he said.

Mullaney reached up and rubbed his jaw where the gun barrel had pressed against it. Fires of hate burned in his eyes, but for the moment they were banked.

"I ain't gonna forget this, Fargo," he growled.

"You'd be well advised to do so," Fargo told him.

Mullaney turned and stalked out of the café, not looking back. He left the empty shotgun behind.

"That is one bad hombre, *ja*," the Norwegian proprietor said.

Fargo holstered his gun. "I'm sorry that happened. I hope Mullaney doesn't come back and try to take any of it out on you."

The woman reached under the counter and brought up an ancient flintlock pistol with a muzzle that flared out like a bell. "We keep this loaded from now on, and if that man comes in again, Papa will shoot him."

"Just be careful," Fargo said. "You don't want to go around shooting anybody if you don't have to." He smiled. "But if you have to . . . don't miss."

He went out the back door, just in case Mullaney had gotten his hands on another gun somehow and was lurking out there. Night had fallen, and the shadows, so plentiful in a town like Saint Louis, could hold many dangers.

As Fargo walked back toward the hotel where he had left the Ovaro, he realized that none of the Trahearne siblings had told him where the boardinghouse was. All he could do was wait for them to show up at the docks tomorrow. They knew where to find the *Rockport*, and he intended to be there when they did.

The Ovaro was still waiting patiently at the hitch rail. Fargo patted the stallion on the shoulder and said, "Sorry, big fella. Things got busy and stayed that way. Let's find a good livery stable stall for you, and a feed bag full of oats."

Once Fargo had tended to his horse's needs, he returned to the hotel. The same clerk was behind the desk. The man recognized Fargo and asked worriedly, "There's not going to be any more trouble, is there?"

"I don't plan on starting any. I just want a room for the night with a comfortable bed."

"We have a couple of vacancies, if . . ."

Fargo knew what the pause meant. "I can afford it," he said. He slapped a coin down on the desk. His cash was dwindling faster than he'd expected, but he thought he still had enough to take care of all his needs before he left Saint Louis.

The clerk's hand swept over the coin, and it was gone. "Very well, sir." He turned the register around. "If you'd care to sign in . . . ?"

Fargo signed his name, left the space for his address blank. His home was wherever he hung his hat, and that was the way it had been for years now. He was sure the day would come when that would change, if he lived long enough, but he couldn't foresee it happening anytime soon.

With his saddlebags slung over his shoulder and carrying the Henry rifle in his left hand, he took the key the clerk gave him and headed upstairs to his room. When he got there and had the door closed, he took out his poke and counted his money, frowning as he realized that he might be a little short after all. For one thing, he didn't know exactly how much Laurie, Cord, and Denny would need to purchase their tickets for the riverboat, and it was more important than ever now that they get out of Saint Louis.

Fargo left the rifle and his other gear in his room and went back downstairs. "I'm looking for a poker game," he told the clerk.

"Try the River Queen Saloon, a couple of blocks down," the man suggested. "I'm told the games there are honest. I wouldn't know myself, since I don't indulge in games of chance."

"Obliged," Fargo said with a curt nod. He didn't like the clerk, and he wouldn't have even if Laurie hadn't said anything about the varmint getting fresh with her. There were too many folks like him in so-called civilization for Fargo's taste.

The River Queen looked like one of Saint Louis's better saloons. Fargo didn't remember it from his last visit, but that wasn't surprising. New saloons were always popping up.

He went inside and found several poker games going on at tables covered with green felt. There weren't any empty chairs at the moment, so Fargo stood at the bar and nursed a beer, keeping an eye on the games until a spot opened up. Then, carrying his beer, he went over to the table, nodded at the empty chair, and asked, "Mind if I sit in?"

A frock-coated man who was probably a professional gambler said, "Help yourself, mister, as long as you've got money."

Fargo took out his poke and set it down on the table hard enough so that the coins inside it clinked together.

The gambler smiled and said, "Ah . . . lovely sound, isn't it?"

"Deal me in," Fargo said.

For the next hour, he played his usual game, not too reckless, not too cautious. He took chances without hesitation when his instincts told him the situation called for it. Mostly, though, he learned the other players, learned which ones could be bluffed, which ones were too timid or too rash for this game. At the end of the hour, he was ahead by a few dollars and ready to step up his game.

So was the man in the frock coat, and for the next hour they traded pots, taking most of the hands, to the disgust of the other players. Fargo was far enough ahead now. When he folded quickly on a hand, he said, "I reckon I'm about done."

The gambler thumbed back his hat on curly black hair and said, "I hate to see you go, friend. You play a good game, and I like to play against the best. My old pappy said that's the way you hone your skills."

"Your pappy was right," Fargo said, "but it's getting late and I rode a good ways today." He pulled his winnings into a pile and started stashing them in the buckskin poke.

"I'm out, too," the gambler said. "Buy you a drink?"

Fargo considered, then smiled and nodded. "Sounds good to me. I'm much obliged."

"Glad to do it. I'm always happy to have some real competition." The gambler smiled at the other men around the table as he stood up. "No offense, boys. If it weren't for you fellas, I might have to look for honest work." He gave a mock shudder at the thought.

The two men went to the bar. The whiskey here at the River Queen was much better than what he'd had at the nameless saloon earlier in the day, Fargo thought.

The gambler licked his lips. "Not as good as the bourbon and branch water back in Kentucky, but not bad, I suppose. Will you be around tomorrow night, friend?"

"I'm afraid not," Fargo replied with a shake of his head. "I'm leaving tomorrow. Heading west."

"Well, I must say I'm not surprised. You look like you're more cut out for the frontier than for civilization. Me, I like a roof over my head at night, and a comfortable bed under me . . . when I can't find a comfortable woman to be under me, that is."

Fargo chuckled. "Civilization does have its advantages at times." He tossed back the rest of his whiskey and set the empty glass on the bar.

"Another?" his newfound friend suggested.

"No, thanks." Fargo slid a coin from his winnings onto the bar. "But you have one on me."

"Very kind of you, sir. I hope the trails are happy ones for you."

"You, too," Fargo said. He lifted a hand in farewell and went to the saloon's entrance, shouldering through the batwings and out into the night.

He was feeling so mellow at the moment that he almost missed the faint scrape of boot leather on the ground to his right. Almost.

But instinct warned him and took over, twisting his body out of the way as a gun roared and Colt flame bloomed in the darkness at the mouth of the alley next to the River Queen. Fargo felt the bullet rip through the air next to his ear. He palmed out the .44 and thumbed off a return shot as he dropped to a knee on the boardwalk in front of the saloon.

Muzzle flame jutted toward him a second time. The slug chewed splinters from the railing at the edge of the boardwalk. That shot was way off, and Fargo knew he had either hit the bushwhacker with his first shot or at least spooked the son of a bitch.

He fired again, and this time he was rewarded by the sight of a man stumbling from the alley mouth out into the street. Enough light came from the windows of the saloon and other nearby buildings so that Fargo was able to see the gun in the man's hand. The would-be killer caught himself, stood swaying as he faced the saloon, and struggled to raise the revolver for a third shot.

Instead, it was Fargo who fired for the third time as the bushwhacker's gun came up. The heavy slug punched into the man's chest and put him down. His gun slipped from lax fingers.

Fargo stood up and jumped off the boardwalk. Even though he didn't think the man was a threat anymore, a couple of fast steps brought him to the bushwhacker's side. He kicked the fallen gun out of reach and covered the man he had shot.

Fargo wasn't surprised at all to see the mustachioed face of Owen Mullaney staring pop-eyed up at him. Mullaney's mouth opened and closed as he gasped for breath that he couldn't quite catch. Air wheezed through the holes in his chest. The spreading bloodstains told Fargo he had hit Mullaney twice in the chest and once lower down on the left side. The man had minutes to live, if that.

"You just couldn't let it go, could you?" Fargo said.

"You . . . you son of a . . . ." Mullaney rasped.

From the boardwalk, someone called, "You all right there, friend?"

Fargo glanced over his shoulder and saw the frock-coated gambler standing there, a derringer in his fist. "Yeah, I'm fine," Fargo told the man. "Somebody better fetch the law, though."

At his feet, Mullaney gasped again, and the rattling

sound of it told Fargo that would be the last time. Sure enough, Mullaney's final breath came out in a long sigh.

"And the undertaker," Fargo added.

Saint Louis had a uniformed police force now, just like the big cities back east. A blue-uniformed constable listened to Fargo's story, which was backed up by the gambler.

"I happened to be looking out through the front door when Fargo left," the man said. "The other fella definitely fired the first shot. That makes it self-defense."

The officer agreed, but said, "There'll have to be an inquest anyway. That's the way we do things now."

The gambler grinned at Fargo and shrugged his shoulders. "Civilization. What can I say?"

Fargo wasn't too happy about the idea of being delayed for an inquest, but there wasn't much he could do about it short of ignoring the law and riding out anyway. He figured he would think about it overnight, since he had to wait until the next day for the Trahearne siblings to leave.

Of course, it wasn't as imperative for them to get out of Saint Louis now, since Owen Mullaney was dead. But Fargo thought it was still a good idea for them to head for Fort Benton as soon as possible. He had a feeling that Cord was likely to get himself and Denny in more trouble if they stayed here. They would stick to the original plan, Fargo decided. He might not even tell them that Mullaney was dead until they were on the riverboat.

Fargo didn't lose any sleep that night over Mullaney's death. The man should have let go of his hatred. Plenty of things in this world were worth dying over, but injured pride wasn't one of them.

After breakfast in the hotel dining room the next morning, Fargo went to the livery stable to saddle up the Ovaro and also bought a packhorse from the liveryman while he was there. Then he rode up the street to a general store and gave the clerk the list of supplies he needed, along with instructions to have them delivered to the livery stable. From there he headed to the docks.

The *Rockport* was a good-looking stern-wheeler, and according to the schedule chalked onto a board next to the door of the shack that served as the dock office, it would be departing at ten o'clock. Dockworkers were loading cargo onto it at the moment, stacking crates on the forward deck.

Fargo noticed several of the men cutting their eyes at him as he tied up the Ovaro, crossed the gangplank, and went aboard. Likely they'd heard what had happened to Mullaney. Some of the men seemed a mite put out, but Fargo thought that others actually looked relieved. Mullaney had probably been pretty quick to enforce his will with his fists.

Fargo found the purser and discovered that there was still one cabin available. Without hesitating, Fargo went ahead and paid for it, all the way to Fort Benton. The Trahearnes could pay him back when they got here. The three of them would be cramped in one cabin, but according to Laurie, they were used to sharing close quarters. Anyway, it would be better than having to sleep out on the deck. That was fine as long as the weather cooperated, but you couldn't count on that happening all the way up the Missouri River.

Fargo left the boat and waited for Laurie, Cord, and Denny, lounging against the thick piling at the foot of the dock where he had tied the Ovaro. That gave him a chance to observe all the activity going on around him. The *Rockport* was hardly the only boat tied up here. Most of them would be heading downstream to New Orleans, and they were taking on cargo and passengers. Other vessels would turn off at Cairo, Illinois, and chug up the Ohio River to Cincinnati, Wheeling, and Pittsburgh. Not too many years earlier, those areas had been the frontier, until men in buckskins and coonskin caps, carrying long-barreled flintlocks and powder horns, had tamed it. If he had been born earlier, he would have been one of those over-the-mountain men, Fargo thought, one of the restless breed who always pushed on into the wilderness.

"There you are," a voice said, bringing him out of his reverie. "I wasn't sure where this boat was docked, so I asked around until I found it."

Fargo turned and saw Laurie Trahearne standing there. She wore a dark blue dress today, instead of the gray one she'd had on the day before, and her red hair was pulled back and tied behind her head. It was a different look, but just as attractive, Fargo thought.

"Where are your brothers?" he asked.

The question brought a frown to Laurie's face. "Aren't they here? They left the boardinghouse before I did. They brought our bags with them . . . not that we have much."

Fargo shook his head. "I haven't seen 'em, and I've been here for a while. I was able to get you a cabin, so you won't have to sleep on deck."

"That's wonderful! Thank you, Mr. Fargo. We'll pay you back. Every penny. It may take a while, but—"

"Don't worry about that now," Fargo said. "We'll talk about it later. Right now, I reckon I should go find those wayward brothers of yours. They may be having trouble finding the boat, and there's only a few minutes until it leaves."

"I'll come with you."

Fargo thought about telling her to go ahead and board the *Rockport*, but he didn't suppose it would do any harm

43

for her to come with him. They started walking along the riverfront. The docks stretched for almost a mile along the western bank of the Mississippi.

They hadn't gone very far before Fargo heard shouts coming from somewhere up ahead. A bad feeling went through him. He had heard a commotion that sounded like that the previous day, just before he saw Cord and Denny for the first time.

Laurie heard it, too. A worried frown appeared on her face. She said, "You don't think that they would . . ."

"We'd better find out," Fargo said.

They walked faster, and soon they came in sight of a large group of men gathered at the foot of one of the docks. As Fargo and Laurie approached, a startled roar went up from the crowd. They parted to allow a backpedaling man to stumble through, clearly out of control. He collapsed after a few feet and lay there only half-conscious, his chest heaving in a ragged rhythm. He was a big man, and as the onlookers stared at him in stunned silence, it was evident that they had never expected to see him knocked out like that.

Cord's voice broke the silence. "Say, that was sure a lucky punch, Denny. There, there, don't carry on. I know you didn't mean to hurt that poor fella."

"Oh, good Lord," Laurie said at Fargo's side. "I thought he'd have more sense than to try something like that again. After everything that went wrong yesterday—"

"Come on, Denny," Cord was saying. "It'll be all right." They moved into sight, making their way through the same gap in the crowd. Cord's head jerked from side to side as he looked around. Fargo knew he was waiting for somebody to offer Denny some sympathy and then remind him of the bets he'd made.

This crowd didn't seem to be in a sympathetic mood, though. In fact, Fargo saw downright angry looks on the faces of some of the men. Suddenly, one of them said in a loud voice, "I saw these two pull the same trick yesterday! It's a cheat! The big one's just playin' dumb!"

Cord said quickly, "That's not true. Denny can't help the way he is—"

"They set us up! Planned to fleece us all!"

"Oh, no," Laurie whispered.

"Get back to the boat," Fargo told her. "Fast."

"What are you going to do?"

With a grim look, Fargo said, "I'll try to get your brothers out of this mess."

"I think I should stay—"

"Go!"

She went, but not without casting several fearful glances over her shoulder as she hurried away toward the dock where the *Rockport* was tied up. Fargo started toward the group of angry men, who had closed in around Cord and Denny before the brothers could get clear of them.

Fargo hoped he could talk some sense into them. After all, they hadn't paid off yet on their bets, so they hadn't lost any money. If he explained that Cord and Denny were leaving Saint Louis, the angry dockworkers might be willing to let them go.

Fargo didn't get a chance to try reasoning with them. One of the men yelled, "I know where I can get a bucket of tar, if you fellas can find some feathers!"

"I say we ride 'em outta town on a rail!" another man shouted.

Cord didn't wait to see what was going to happen. He said, "Denny, get us out of here!"

Without a word, Denny followed his brother's order and plowed into the crowd. His long, powerful arms and keglike fists lashed out right and left. Angry shouts rose as men began to fall under those sledgehammer blows.

Denny picked up one of the men he'd knocked down and used the hombre as a battering ram, charging forward to clear an even wider path through the crowd. Cord was right behind him.

Fargo saw it all happening, but there wasn't a blasted thing he could do to stop it. Denny burst out of the melee with Cord following him. They dashed toward Fargo, who could tell that Denny was holding back so his long legs wouldn't make him outrun Cord.

"Go!" Fargo shouted to them, waving them on. "Laurie's waiting for you! Look for her!"

As they ran past, he stepped between them and the furious mob, drawing his Colt as he did so. He leveled the revolver at the onrushing dockworkers and eared back the hammer. The men slid to a frantic halt about twenty feet away. Fargo knew that facing a .44 from that distance was sort of like staring down the barrel of a cannon.

"Hold it right there," Fargo told them.

"Those two bastards tried to cheat us!" one of the men yelled.

"Yeah, but they didn't get away with it," Fargo said. "You haven't lost any money."

"I did yesterday!" another man said. "Damn flimflam artists!"

"Just let 'em go. They're leaving town. They won't bother any of you again."

"They deserve a good tar an' featherin'!" Shouts of agreement rose from the mob.

"Most folks never get what they really deserve," Fargo said, "and most of them are lucky that they don't. Go on back to your jobs and forget about what happened here."

A member of the mob sneered at him. "What're you gonna do, mister? Shoot all of us? That'll be a good trick, seein' as how there's twenty or thirty of us and only five or six rounds in that gun of yours." He turned to the others. "Let's rush him!"

"You're right," Fargo said. "So if you rush me, only five or six of you will die. *And you'll sure be one of them, mister.*"

The crowd had started to surge forward. Fargo's cold words stopped them in their tracks again. He wasn't going to gun down anyone in cold blood, but they didn't have to know that.

He started backing away. The men watched him but didn't make any move to come after him. That might have worked—if one of the workers on a dock he passed hadn't suddenly thrown an empty crate at him. It smashed heavily against Fargo's shoulder and made him stagger to the side. The Colt slipped out of his hand and skittered away.

"Get him!" somebody howled.

Fargo lunged after his gun and managed to snatch it off the ground, but the mob was already on him. Hands caught at his clothes. Fists pounded into him. He lashed out with the gun and smashed it against a man's skull. His left fist connected with another man's jaw and bought him a little breathing room.

That respite would last only a second, he knew. Then the mob would overwhelm him, beat him to the ground, maybe even stomp the life out of him.

Before that could happen, a hurricane of punches struck the crowd. Denny battered men aside, picked them up and threw them into other men like he was playing ninepins. "Laurie sent me to get you, Mr. Fargo!" he shouted. "She said for me to bring you to the boat! It's leaving!"

That was their best chance for survival, Fargo realized. If the *Rockport* had steam up and was pulling away from the dock, he and Denny could escape from the mob by leaping aboard before it got too far into the river. Not just their best chance, he thought as they broke away from the mob and sprinted along the waterfront—probably their *only* chance.

The shrill cry of a steam whistle told him that the riverboat was under way. He spotted its stacks up ahead. There was already a gap between the wharf and the deck, but it was still narrow enough for them to leap over it. It wouldn't be for much longer, though. He poured on the speed and panted, "Don't hold back on my account, Denny! Get on that boat!"

"I'm runnin' . . . as hard as I can . . . Mr. Fargo!"

As they neared the dock, Fargo saw the Ovaro tied to the piling where he had been leaning earlier. If he stopped to untie the stallion, the mob would catch them. He had another idea, though.

Their boots pounded on the planks of the dock. Fargo saw Laurie and Cord on board the boat, shouting encouragement to them. The big paddle at the stern revolved slowly, picking up speed as it churned through the water.

"Jump for it!" Fargo shouted to Denny, then left the edge of the dock in a flying leap that carried him high in the air as he put all his strength and momentum behind it.

For a second he thought he wasn't going to make it. The river loomed below him. He wasn't worried about drowning, since he could swim like a fish, but he knew that if he fell into the Mississippi, the mob would be waiting for him when he climbed out.

Those thoughts took only an instant. Then he cleared the edge of the deck and plunged forward, landing painfully among some of the cargo. Denny crashed down beside him.

They had made it.

The Ovaro was still on shore, though, and as Fargo

clambered to his feet he looked back and saw the big black-and-white stallion throwing his head up and down. The horse knew that Fargo was leaving without him and didn't like it.

Neither did Fargo. He put two fingers in his mouth and whistled sharply.

The Ovaro jerked his head up harder than before. Fargo always tied the reins loosely so that the horse could get loose if he had to. The reins came free now, and as the *Rockport* turned in the water and began to steam upriver, the Ovaro turned and ran along the dock.

Laurie and Cord reached Fargo and Denny. "My God, are you all right?" Laurie cried.

"I'm fine," Denny said. "I got Mr. Fargo like you told me to, Laurie."

Crying, she hugged him.

"What's that horse doing?" Cord asked Fargo.

"You'll see," the Trailsman said.

On shore, dockworkers leaped out of the way of the galloping stallion. The Ovaro pulled ahead of the riverboat. Up ahead was a long wharf that stretched a good distance out into the river. Cord looked from the horse to the wharf and back again, then said, "You can't mean that he's going to . . ."

"Hide and watch," Fargo said with a smile.

Barely slowing, the Ovaro thundered out onto the dock, causing more men to scatter. Some of them had to dive into the river to avoid being trampled by the stallion. The Ovaro stretched out, running hard.

Fargo hoped the timing was right. There was some open space on the deck at the stern, in front of the paddlewheel. If the stallion missed . . .

Fargo wasn't going to think about that.

The riverboat's passengers lined the railings to watch the desperate race. Some of them later told Fargo what happened next was the most amazing thing they had ever seen. It was right up there, Fargo had to admit.

Because the Ovaro still didn't slow down as it came to the end of the dock. Instead, the stallion leaped into the air, sailing out over the water, forehooves extended, aiming like an arrow at the *Rockport* as it steamed past.

Then the iron shoes on those hooves crashed against the deck planks. Momentum carried the Ovaro forward. Fargo was there to grab the reins, and so was Denny. They helped the big horse stay up as he skidded to a halt at the far edge of the deck.

Thunderous cheers went up from the passengers. Angry curses came from the shore as the members of the mob stood there shaking their fists at the riverboat. Laurie was laughing and crying at the same time as she threw her arms around Fargo's neck.

"That was incredible!" she said. "I never saw anything like it!"

"Be all right with me if I never have to see anything like it again," Fargo said with a grin as he stroked the Ovaro's shoulder. The horse was trembling a little but seemed all right. The important thing was that they were still together, even though he had lost his saddlebags, his rifle, and the supplies he had bought earlier. Those things could be replaced. The Ovaro couldn't.

Anyway, he thought, he could get off the boat somewhere upstream and ride back to Saint Louis, maybe even reclaim his gear.

Except for the fact that Laurie was still hugging him and saying, "Now that you're on board, you'll come with us, won't you, Skye?"

"Yeah, Mr. Fargo," Denny said. "Come with us."

Even Cord shrugged and said, "We'd have been goners without you. Might as well stay on board."

Fargo was tempted. But he probably still would have

followed his original plan had he not glanced up at that moment and seen the blonde smiling down at him from the riverboat's texas deck.

"Looks like I'm going to Fort Benton," the Trailsman said.

4

The wind fluttered cornsilk curls around the woman's slightly rounded face. She wore a high-necked, blue and silver gown with bursts of white lace at the throat and cuffs. From this angle, it was difficult for Fargo to tell how tall she was, but he had a feeling she was tall. Well built, too, with broad shoulders and breasts that thrust out as if they were challenging a man to take hold of them. Full, red lips curved in the smile she directed at Fargo. He felt like he ought to raise a hand and acknowledge her, but before he could do that, she turned away from the railing around the texas deck, which she had gripped with long, slender fingers, and disappeared.

Agreeing to travel to Fort Benton on this riverboat just because a good-looking woman had smiled at him was the sort of whim that Fargo seldom if ever indulged in. But it was a whim that had gotten him in this mess to start with, he reminded himself. On two separate occasions, he could have ridden away and had nothing more to do with Cord and Denny. But both times he had given in to impulse.

Sometimes a man just had to follow his heart, he thought. Even when it got him into trouble.

"What are you looking at up there, Skye?" Laurie asked. She must not have noticed the blonde. And evidently she had decided that it was all right to call him Skye, too.

Fargo shook his head. "Nothing," he lied. "Just looking at the pilothouse."

He was a truthful man by nature, but he was also smart enough to know it wouldn't be wise to tell one attractive woman that he was impressed by another attractive woman. He hadn't lived as long as he had by being a fool.

"I never saw a horse on a boat before," Denny said. "Is it all right for him to ride on here?"

Fargo chuckled. "I imagine the captain will have something to say about that. And unless I miss my guess, that's him coming now."

A portly man in a black suit and a riverman's cap was on his way down the stairs from the upper decks. He had a white goatee, and his face was deeply tanned by years of being out here on the river. When he reached the main deck, he strode toward them.

"Who does this . . . this animal belong to?" he demanded.

"The big fella's mine," Fargo said as he stood there with a hand still on the stallion's shoulder.

"You can't bring a horse on this boat! We don't have the facilities for livestock!"

"I've seen plenty of horses on riverboats before," Fargo pointed out. "Mules and cattle and oxen, too. Not to mention pigs and sheep. One horse won't cause any trouble, Captain. You *are* the captain?"

"F. X. MacGuinness, sir, master of the *Rockport*."

"Name's Skye Fargo, and like I said, this is my horse. I'll be responsible for him."

Captain F. X. MacGuinness snorted. "You most certainly will." He frowned as something occurred to him. "Do *you* have a ticket, Mr. Fargo? I was watching as you, ah, *boarded* at the last minute."

"I can pay my way," Fargo said, "and since I happen to know that you don't have any cabins available, I'll be happy to sleep back here with my horse."

"So you don't have a ticket?"

Fargo shrugged. "Not yet."

"I could have you thrown off this boat, you know," MacGuinness blustered. "You and your horse both."

Laurie spoke up, saying, "Please don't do that, Captain. The only reason Mr. Fargo is on board is because he was trying to help my brothers and me. If it weren't for him, that mob back there on the docks might have killed my brothers."

MacGuinness frowned. "Yes, I know. As I told you, I saw the disturbance." He looked at Fargo. "Your name is familiar, sir. Skye Fargo, you said?"

"He's the Trailsman," Cord supplied helpfully.

The riverboat captain's frown disappeared, replaced by a look of surprise. "Of course! I've heard a great deal about you, Mr. Fargo." A canny expression appeared on his face. "Now I understand. I must say, you drew more attention to yourself than I thought you would. But I suppose how you do things is up to you." MacGuinness put out his hand. "We can carry your horse, of course. And I'll see what I can do about finding a cabin for you, so you won't have to sleep on the deck. Unless you prefer to."

Fargo shook hands with the man and said, "No, that's all right. I don't want to put anybody out, though."

"That's quite all right." MacGuinness looked at Laurie, Cord, and Denny. "And these are associates of yours?"

"Friends," Fargo said.

"Of course. Friends."

And then damned if the captain didn't wink at him, like they shared some great secret.

"I have to get back to the pilothouse," MacGuinness went on. "Make yourself comfortable, Mr. Fargo. I'm sure I'll see you later."

With that, the captain went back to the stairs and started up. Behind him, Laurie frowned at Fargo and asked, "What in the world was *that* all about? His attitude changed as soon as he realized that you're the Trailsman."

Cord said, "He's just glad to have a famous man on his boat. It's good for business."

Fargo didn't think that was it at all. Something else was going on here, but for the life of him, he couldn't figure out what it was.

Like those old boys at Troy, though, in the storybooks about ancient Greece and the like, he wasn't going to look a gift horse in the mouth. He just hoped he wouldn't end up like them.

One thing was for sure, though—that blonde he had seen earlier on the texas deck was pretty enough to make a fella launch a thousand ships or burn the topless towers of Ilium . . .

The purser had told Fargo which cabin would belong to the Trahearnes for the duration of the trip upriver. They found it on the second deck. Cord was carrying a couple of small bags. In all the confusion, Fargo hadn't even noticed them. Cord set the bags down and said, "You take the bed, Laurie. Denny and I can sleep on the floor."

"That's not fair," Laurie said. "You always sleep on the floor."

Denny grinned. "I'm used to it. I don't like to sleep in a bed no more."

Laurie stroked his arm and said, "Things will be different one of these days, Denny. I promise. We'll have a real home, with a room for each of us."

"I don't know if I'd like that," Denny replied with a worried frown. "I might get scared if I had to sleep in a room by myself."

Fargo excused himself and left to let them get settled in. He had unsaddled the Ovaro and left the stallion tied on the rear deck. Nobody would bother him, and anyone foolish enough to try would regret it. The stallion was a one-man horse.

Fargo walked up to the texas deck. The salon was there, and even though it wasn't the middle of the day yet, he was thinking about having a drink. He decided that a cup of coffee might be better, though.

When he walked into the salon, he saw that heavy curtains were pulled over the windows, making it dim inside the room. Even so, he had no trouble seeing the woman sitting alone at one of the tables. She seemed to shine with a light of her own, and the glow became even brighter when she looked up at him and smiled.

"I was hoping I'd run into you," she said in a low, husky voice. "Sit down and join me."

It was phrased as a command, not a request, and even though by nature Fargo didn't cotton all that much to taking orders, he pulled back a chair and sat down.

She was laying out a hand of solitaire, her fingers moving with deft grace. Fargo had a feeling she could make the cards sing and dance under her touch. With a faint smile still on her lips, she finished laying them out and started dealing, lowering her eyes to the baize-covered table as she began placing and moving the cards.

"You're Skye Fargo," she said.

"Guilty as charged. Have we met?" He knew they hadn't. Beyond a shadow of a doubt, he would have remembered it if they had.

"No, but I've heard about you. You match your description. And it would take someone as audacious as the Trailsman to face down an angry mob with only a six-gun."

Fargo chuckled. "Yeah, well, that didn't work out too well, did it?"

"You're still alive," she pointed out, "and so are your friends."

"That's true. You watched the whole thing?"

"As much of it as I could from where I was. It was quite thrilling."

"Not as much so when you're right in the middle of it and about to get stomped," Fargo said.

"I suppose not." She looked up from the cards and extended a hand across the table. "Alexis Rimbard."

Fargo took her hand. It was smooth and cool, and yet heat seemed to flow from it that traced a fiery path along his nerves until it reached his core and kindled a blaze there. It seemed to pulse in time with his heart, or maybe just the throb of the engines.

He didn't show that as he said, "It's my pleasure, ma'am."

"Given time, perhaps an even greater one," she murmured. She returned her attention to the game, at least on the surface. After a moment, she asked, "Who were those people with you?"

"Some folks I met in Saint Louis."

"Friends of yours?"

"Well, I'd say so," Fargo replied, although in the case of Cord Trahearne, that was stretching things a mite, he thought.

"The young woman was quite attractive, that red hair and all."

Fargo didn't say anything. He was still too canny to rise to the bait.

"Why was that mob after the two young men?" Alexis asked.

Fargo explained about the trick Cord and Denny played. Alexis laughed in delight.

"A couple of boys after my own heart," she said. "People mean enough and greedy enough to fall for a trick like that deserve to lose their money."

"Spoken like a true gambler," Fargo said.

"That's exactly what I am ... but you already knew that from the way I handle the cards, didn't you?"

"I had a pretty good idea," Fargo said.

"Do you play?"

"Poker," Fargo said. "Among other things." If she could make suggestive comments, so could he.

Abruptly, Alexis swept the columns of cards together without finishing the game. "One hand of showdown," she suggested as she shuffled.

"All right," Fargo said. "What are the stakes?"

"If you win, I have dinner with you tonight."

"And if you win?"

"I haven't decided yet."

"A man would have to be a fool to agree to a wager like that."

Alexis finished shuffling and set the deck in front of Fargo. "Or a man who believed in his luck," she said. "Cut?"

Fargo didn't hesitate. He reached out and cut the cards.

Alexis restacked them, dealt Fargo the eight of hearts, face up. "Hearts," she murmured. She dropped the three of clubs in front of her.

"Got you beat so far," Fargo said.

"The game's just starting."

Fargo's next card was the two of diamonds. "Not so good," he said.

Alexis dealt herself the seven of hearts. "You're still winning."

"Like you said, the game's just started."

The eight of spades landed in front of Fargo. "A pair," Alexis said. She gave herself the six of diamonds. "It's looking good for you, Skye. You don't mind if I call you Skye, do you?"

"Not at all," Fargo replied.

"And your next card is . . . jack of hearts. Better and better." Alexis laid the six of clubs in front of her. "A pair, but not as good as yours. One card to go, Skye. Would you like to increase the stakes?"

"Hard to do when I still don't know what you're playing for."

She smiled. "Yes, it is, isn't it?" She dealt the king of spades to him. "Quite the gentleman, but he's all alone. Still, your eights beat my sixes." She turned the next card and placed it in front of her. "Or at least . . . they did."

The six of spades lay next to the rest of her cards, giving her a third six. Fargo grinned and pushed his cards in. "You win," he said. "You ever figure out what you were playing for?"

"I did," she said. "Since I won, *you're* going to have dinner with *me*."

Fargo laughed out loud. "You could've just asked me."

"You could have just asked me," she pointed out. "But it was more fun this way, wasn't it?"

Fargo had to admit it was. "What time?"

"Here in the salon at eight o'clock."

"I'll be here," he promised.

Alexis started shuffling the cards again. "You'd better be," she said. "I can't abide a man who welshes on his bets."

Alexis left the salon while Fargo was still sitting at the table drinking the cup of coffee that the steward on duty had brought to him. Fargo called the man over again and said, "You know anything about the lady who just left here?"

"You mean Miss Rimbard? Sure, she's traveled with us several times before. She's a regular on the riverboats."

"Professional gambler?"

The steward shrugged. "All I've ever seen her do is

play cards with the fellas, mister. She don't take them back to her cabin, if that's what you're asking."

It wasn't, but Fargo supposed the question might have been in the back of his mind. Alexis hadn't struck him as a prostitute, though, and he was glad that his judgment appeared to have been sound.

"She seems like the sort of lady who would be more at home on the New Orleans run, instead of heading out into the frontier."

"I think that's where she's from originally. Maybe there was some sort of trouble that forced her to leave. Be a real shame if that was true. She's as nice as she can be."

Fargo thought so, too. He recalled meeting a lady gambler on a riverboat down in Texas who had been running away from a troubled past in New Orleans. He hoped that Alexis didn't have anything that dark in her background.

Fargo was about finished with his coffee when one of the passengers came into the salon. The man was tall and well built, wearing high-topped boots, whipcord trousers, a gray wool shirt with a brown vest over it, and a brown, flat-crowned hat. A revolver with well-worn walnut grips rode in a holster on his hip. He looked around the room, spotted Fargo, and stalked over to the table.

"You're Fargo?" he demanded.

Fargo had taken an instant dislike to this hombre, and the man's sharp tone didn't do anything to convince Fargo he'd made a mistake. "Depends on who's asking," he returned coolly.

The man pulled out one of the other chairs at the table and sat down without asking. "The captain told me you were on board," he said. "What the hell is going on here? Am I still in command or not?"

Fargo made an effort not to look flabbergasted by the questions. He faced the man squarely across the table and said, "Mister, I don't have the slightest idea what in the blue blazes you're talking about."

The stranger frowned, obviously torn as to whether he believed Fargo or not. After a moment, he said, "General Basswood didn't send you?"

"I don't know General Basswood from a wooden Indian's ass," Fargo replied honestly.

Evidently the man had decided to believe what Fargo said, because he looked stricken and muttered, "Oh, good Lord, what have I done?"

"You tell me," Fargo suggested.

Instead, the man shoved back his chair, stood up hurriedly, and said, "Please, sir, pay no attention to anything I just said." Before Fargo could respond, the man turned and walked out of the salon, leaving Fargo staring after him in complete confusion.

Well, maybe not quite complete, Fargo amended. He had the glimmering of an idea. With that in mind, he finished his coffee and went to look for the captain.

As he emerged onto the deck, he saw the man he had just been talking to standing with MacGuinness at the railing. They were engaged in a spirited conversation, but they fell silent as they both spotted Fargo. The stranger turned and stalked off, heading down the stairs to the lower decks. Fargo walked over to MacGuinness.

"Captain," Fargo said. "I reckon that hombre was giving you an earful."

Keeping his voice pitched low, MacGuinness asked the same thing the stranger had. "General Basswood didn't send you?"

"I'll tell you what I told him. I don't know any General Basswood."

"Then what *are* you doing here?"

"Exactly what it looked like," Fargo said. "Avoiding a mob that would have tarred and feathered me, at best, or

61

stomped me to death if they felt like it." He smiled thinly. "But you thought the army sent me to protect some of the cargo you're carrying, didn't you?"

It was a guess, but the startled look in MacGuinness's eyes told Fargo that he was right. MacGuinness glanced away and said, "I really shouldn't say more."

"What is it?" Fargo persisted. "Guns? Money? I can't think of anything else that would get anybody as worked up as that other gent was."

"I have nothing more to say," MacGuinness muttered as he turned away.

"If you're expecting trouble, Captain, it might be a good idea to let me in on it," Fargo suggested. "I might be able to help you."

MacGuinness just shook his head as he hurried toward the stairs leading up to the pilothouse.

To his back, Fargo asked, "Does this mean I have to sleep with my horse after all?"

The captain didn't answer.

Fargo wasn't sure whether to be amused or worried. Everything he had seen and heard so far indicated that the *Rockport* was carrying something important for the army, something that was supposed to be a secret. The stiff-necked stranger was probably an officer who had been sent along to guard the shipment, whatever it was. Fargo still leaned toward rifles, or maybe a payroll. There were probably some enlisted men on board, too, traveling in civilian clothes like their commander.

They had nothing to fear from Fargo. He had worked with the army on numerous occasions in the past, as was well known on the frontier. That knowledge was what had led Captain MacGuinness to assume that the army had sent him here to help guard the shipment, Fargo supposed. MacGuinness had told the officer about it, and that was what had provoked the confrontation in the salon.

Fargo stood at the railing for a moment, mulling over the situation, then shook his head and put it out of his mind for the time being. He had other things to think about, like his dinner engagement with Alexis Rimbard that evening.

"There you are, Skye," Laurie said from behind him.

He turned toward her and smiled. "You and your brothers get settled in all right?"

She nodded. "Yes, I think we'll be quite comfortable. I can't thank you enough for getting us out of Saint Louis before that awful man could come after us again."

"About that," Fargo said. "I never got a chance to tell you until now, but Mullaney tried to bushwhack me last night."

"Oh, no! What happened?"

"He's dead."

Laurie looked surprised. "Dead?" she repeated.

"Yeah. He didn't give me much choice in the matter." He told her about the gunfight in front of the River Queen Saloon, then concluded by saying, "I was supposed to attend the inquest, but I reckon they'll just have to carry on without me."

"Will that get you in trouble with the law?"

"Not enough to worry about," Fargo assured her. "There's at least one witness to testify that the killing was in self-defense, and I've got a feeling Mullaney didn't have a very good reputation in Saint Louis. The coroner may not be happy when I don't show up, but everyone will have forgotten about it by the time I get back to Saint Louis. That may be a while."

Laurie rested her hands on the railing and sighed. "I'm sorry we brought all this trouble down on your head, Skye."

"You and your brothers aren't to blame at all. It was my decision to get involved in your problems."

"That's because you're a good man," she said as she turned to him. "Thanks to you, I'm starting to believe that such things really do exist."

She might not feel that way if she knew how he'd reacted to Alexis. But Fargo wasn't going to tell her, so it was entirely possible she would never find out about it.

"You'll have dinner with us tonight, won't you, Skye?"

Now there was a complication he hadn't counted on. He said, "I may not be able to do that."

The disappointment that appeared on her face bothered him. "Why not?"

Fargo couldn't come up with a legitimate reason, so he said, "Well, now, come to think of it, I reckon I can after all."

He would just have to be careful not to eat too much, since he planned on having dinner with Alexis a little later.

"I saw you talking to the captain. Did you ever find out why he was acting so strange earlier?"

"Not really," Fargo said, which was pretty much true. He had ideas, but no one had confirmed them yet.

"I'm just glad he didn't make you get off the boat. I think the trip to Fort Benton will be a lot more enjoyable with you along. And when we get there, if we can't find Pa, you can help us look for him, like you said you would."

Fargo nodded. He wasn't going back on the promise he had made to the Trahearne siblings. He would find Isaac Trahearne. Of course, it was possible that the man was dead. Fargo hoped that wouldn't turn out to be the case, but either way, Laurie, Cord, and Denny deserved to know the truth.

"It's pretty country, isn't it?" she said as she stood at the railing, watching the rolling green hills drift by as the *Rockport* continued chugging upriver. Soon, the stern-wheeler would reach the spot where the Missouri flowed into the Mississippi and would make the westward turn.

"It's pretty here," Fargo said, "but before we get to Fort Benton we'll be going through some mighty ugly country. The river's not too pretty, either. There's a reason some call it the Big Muddy."

Fargo paused. He should have made sure before Laurie and her brothers left Saint Louis that they knew what they were getting into. It was too late to turn back now, but he supposed he ought to warn her anyway.

"There could be danger, too," he said. "There are a few outposts like Fort Benton, but for the most part we're leaving civilization behind. Indians have been known to attack riverboats, and so have outlaw gangs."

He didn't mention that the mysterious cargo on board the *Rockport* might also serve as a magnet for river pirates, if they got wind of it. That was probably why Captain MacGuinness and that stiff-necked army officer were being so secretive about it.

"I'm not worried," Laurie said with a shake of her head. "The boys and I are used to taking care of ourselves. Anyway, we've got you along to help us, don't we, Skye?"

His hands were resting on the railing, too. She moved her left hand over and laid it on top of his right hand. Once she had decided it was all right to trust him, she had warmed up pretty quickly. That could prove to be a complication before the trip upriver was completed.

"We ought to be safe enough," Fargo said. "The crew is well armed, and most of the men on board probably have guns and know how to use them, too." Including, he suspected, a detail of army troopers.

"I'm just glad to leave Saint Louis behind. I didn't like it much, and I sure didn't like working at that hotel. There were too many temptations there for Cord and Denny, too."

"They'd better not try the same sort of tricks they were pulling back there while they're on this boat," Fargo warned her. "There's no place to run here if folks get mad at them. And it won't be much better once we get to Fort Benton."

"Don't worry," Laurie said. "They've put those days behind them."

Fargo hoped that was true. He wasn't sure he had as much confidence in her brothers as Laurie did, though. Especially where Cord was concerned.

"Look!" she said suddenly, pointing up ahead. "Is that the Missouri River?"

Fargo smiled as he saw the broad opening where the two rivers merged. "It sure is."

"We're really on our way now, aren't we? There's no turning back."

"No," Fargo said. Laurie had just unknowingly echoed the thought he'd had earlier. "No turning back."

5

There was nothing fancy about the dining room on most riverboats, either in furnishings or in the food served there. It was simple fare, based around things that would travel well—salt pork, potatoes, biscuits. From time to time, when a boat stopped to take on wood for the engine's fireboxes, members of the crew would go ashore to hunt. It was a treat when they came back with a deer or an elk. Fresh meat was always welcome on a riverboat headed up the Missouri, where scores of miles could pass without any settlements.

Since the *Rockport* had left Saint Louis just that morning, the cook still had beef in the larder, as well as some fresh vegetables. As Fargo sat on a bench next to one of the tables with Laurie, Cord, and Denny that evening, he warned them not to expect such appetizing meals all the way to Fort Benton.

"By the time we get there, you'll be sick to death of salt pork," he told them with a smile. "But it'll keep you from starving to death."

"We've been closer to that more times than I like to think about, back on the farm," Laurie said.

"Damn Pa, anyway, for running off and leaving us like that," Cord said.

Laurie glared at him. "Cord, you hush that kind of talk! Pa did what he thought best. He thought he stood a better chance of making something of himself on the frontier. He just wanted to be able to give all of us a better life."

"Sure he did," Cord said around a mouthful of roast beef. "The fact that he hated working on the farm from dawn to dusk didn't have anything to do with it, did it?"

"I liked plowing," Denny said. "I liked the mules."

"The mules went with the rest of the farm to pay the taxes. They're probably dead by now."

Denny looked like he wanted to cry, and Laurie glared at Cord again. "Why do you have to say things like that?" she demanded. "You know he gets upset easy."

"It's all right," Denny told her. He sighed. "I know things never stay good for very long. I'm dumb, but I'm not *that* dumb."

Laurie looked daggers at Cord, who just shrugged as if to say it wasn't his fault. Fargo figured they squabbled a lot. Most brothers and sisters he'd been around did.

Denny's attention didn't stay on any one thing for very long, so a moment later he asked, "Will there be wild Indians where we're going, Mr. Fargo?"

"There could be," Fargo said. "They're not very likely to bother the riverboat, though, and the ones who come around Fort Benton are mostly tame."

"Mostly?" Cord repeated.

"It pays to keep an eye on the folks around you," Fargo said, "and that goes for white men as well as red. Most of the people you'll run into on the frontier are as honest as the day is long. It's the few who aren't that you have to watch out for."

"Indians kind of scare me," Denny said.

Laurie patted his hand. "Don't you worry. As long as Mr. Fargo's looking out for us, I'm sure he won't let anything bad happen."

That was a hell of a lot of faith she was putting in him, he thought, and he wasn't sure he liked it. He was just a man; he couldn't keep everything bad in the world from happening, no matter how hard he tried.

"I've been thinking," Cord said, changing the subject. "Some of the crew I've seen are pretty big fellas. I'll bet they like to fight every now and then—"

"Cord, stop it," Laurie said. "Don't you even think about trying that trick on any of them. What would you do if they got mad and came after you, like that mob back in Saint Louis? Here on the boat, you wouldn't be able to get away from them." She shook her head in dismay. "It hasn't even been a day yet! Have you already forgotten what almost happened?"

"The only reason we had trouble in Saint Louis was because I got a little too greedy," Cord argued. "We tried it too soon and too close to where we'd been working the day before. That's why somebody who remembered us was in the crowd. But nobody on board this boat knows us, especially the crew."

"Remember what I said a minute ago about having to watch out for the folks who aren't honest?" Fargo asked. "You don't want to fall into that category, Cord."

The young man flushed angrily. "There's nothing dishonest about trying to take care of your family the best way you know how."

"I'm sure that's what your father was trying to do when he left Ohio."

Cord pushed back his empty plate and stood up. "You don't know anything about it," he snapped. "You weren't there."

"Cord, wait," Laurie said, but he didn't listen to her. He turned and walked stiffly out of the dining room.

"Reckon I poked my nose into family business," Fargo said. "Sorry."

Laurie shook her head. "It's not your fault, Skye. Cord's always been that way. He's got a chip on his shoulder, especially where Pa's concerned, and he always looks for the easy way out, even when it just leads to more trouble."

The atmosphere at the table was subdued as Fargo, Laurie, and Denny finished their meal. Then Laurie said, "I suppose we'd better go see if we can find Cord. I don't think he'll get into any trouble, but you can't ever tell."

"I need to go check on my horse," Fargo said. "If I see Cord anywhere around, I'll tell him that you're looking for him."

"Thank you."

Laurie smiled at him, then took Denny's hand and led the young giant out of the dining room. Fargo strolled back along the deck to the rear of the boat, where the Ovaro nickered happily to see him. Before dinner, Fargo had found a bucket for water and another for grain and filled them both. The stallion wouldn't like being cooped up on the boat, though. Fargo planned to take him ashore and let him stretch his legs every time the *Rockport* stopped for wood.

When he was satisfied that the Ovaro was all right for the time being, he walked toward the bow. The cargo area up there was stacked high with crates and barrels and kegs, and he found several passengers sitting among them, using kegs for seats and playing cards on a blanket spread over the top of a crate. The sun had set, but there was enough light left in the sky for them to be able to see the cards.

They saw Fargo, too, and he noticed how they kept an eye on him without being too obvious about it. He took note of the guns on their hips as well. Despite the civilian clothes they wore, he was convinced they were enlisted men. One of the card players, a burly, middle-aged fellow with a bald head, was probably their sergeant.

Fargo didn't linger, although he was curious about what

he might find if he started opening some of those crates. It was none of his business, he knew, but at the same time, if the boat was carrying something that might attract trouble, he wanted to be ready for it.

Maybe he ought to talk to Captain MacGuinness and the officer in charge of the guard detail, he thought, and offer his services. It wouldn't be the first time he had performed such a chore, and this time the army wouldn't even have to pay him.

However, at the moment he had another engagement, and he was eager to keep it. He headed up to the texas deck and went into the salon.

Alexis wasn't there, but the steward working behind the bar caught his eye and motioned him over. The man said, "Miss Rimbard asked me to tell you that she'll be here in a few minutes, Mr. Fargo." He pointed to a table in the corner. "You'll be having dinner over there."

The meal he had shared with the Trahearnes had blunted Fargo's appetite, but he thought he could still eat a little. He nodded his thanks and went to sit down at the table, which was covered with a fine linen cloth and set for two diners, including glasses and a bottle of wine.

He figured that Alexis wanted to make an entrance, to show off for him a little, and when she came into the salon a few minutes later, he was sure of it. She wore a beautiful gown of faded rose, cut low enough so that the creamy swells of her breasts were visible. The sleeves left her arms bare as well. That was a lot of beautiful flesh on display, and Fargo appreciated every inch of it.

He came to his feet as she strolled over to the table. Obviously, she was aware that the eyes of every man in the room were following her. And since she was the only woman in the salon, that meant she was the object of plenty of male attention.

"Skye," she murmured as she held out a hand to him.

He took it and said, "You look lovely."

It was true. She had piled her blond hair on top of her head tonight in an elaborate arrangement of curls that made her seem even taller. Her eyes were almost on a level with Fargo's to begin with. He held on to her hand for a second or two longer than he had to, because he felt that same heat coursing from her and enjoyed it.

"No games tonight?" he asked as they sat down. "You've got a salon full of admirers here who would love to sit across a poker table from you."

"They might not enjoy it so much when I cleaned them out," she said with a laugh.

"You're confident that you'd win?"

"Always. Why else would I play?" She picked up one of the glasses of wine that had been waiting on the table and sipped from it. "But to answer your question . . . no, no games tonight. Tonight I'm very serious."

"Poker's a serious business for a professional," Fargo pointed out.

"Yes, and I think you'd make a worthy opponent in a real game. Perhaps another time."

Fargo lifted his glass. "I'll drink to that."

The steward brought over their meals. Fargo was aware of the envious glances of the other men in the room. Most of them were well dressed, probably on their way upriver on business, while Fargo still wore his buckskins. More than likely, every man in here wished he could take Fargo's place across the table from Alexis, so that he could look into her beautiful, pale blue eyes and hear her throaty laugh. Fargo knew that he was certainly enjoying her company.

He had a feeling he would enjoy it even more before the night was over, too. The attraction between them was a palpable thing, so thick and strong he could almost reach out and touch it.

The food was the same sort he'd had earlier in the dining room. Alexis just picked at her plate and didn't really seem all that interested in eating. That was fine with Fargo, because it meant she didn't notice that he wasn't eating much, either.

The door into the salon opened, and Cord Trahearne came in. He went to the bar and ordered a drink, glanced over and gave Fargo a curt nod. Fargo had told Laurie that if he saw Cord, he'd tell him that she was looking for him, but he didn't want to get up from the table and be rude to Alexis. Anyway, as long as Cord was just sitting there at the bar, maybe he wouldn't get into any trouble. When Fargo left the salon, he would try to snatch a second to speak to the young man.

Meanwhile, he returned his attention to Alexis.

A few minutes later, Captain MacGuinness came into the salon, looked around, and then came toward the table. He took off his cap as he stopped beside them. With a smile, he said, "Good evening, Miss Rimbard."

"Captain," she said. Fargo thought she was a little annoyed by the interruption, but she smiled politely. "What can I do for you?"

"Actually, I was looking for Mr. Fargo here." He turned to Fargo and went on, "I promised I'd see about finding a cabin for you, and I have."

"That's not absolutely necessary," Fargo said. "I don't want to put anybody out."

"You won't be. There's a small cabin down at the other end of this deck that wasn't claimed by the man who booked passage in it. He never showed up. I don't know what happened to him, but it doesn't matter. The cabin is yours if you want it."

Fargo nodded. "I'm much obliged, Captain. I've slept on boat decks before. A cabin is better."

"Indeed it is," MacGuinness agreed. "It's the last door

on the right, on the starboard side." He put his cap on, gave the brim a tug, and said, "Good night."

When MacGuinness was gone, Fargo said, "The captain seems like a nice fella."

"He is," Alexis said. "I know most of the captains whose boats travel the Missouri, and he's one of the best. But enough about him." She reached across the table and clasped Fargo's hand. "Skye, do you have the same idea I do about how we ought to spend the rest of this evening?"

Fargo smiled. "I reckon I do. Some folks would say it's a mite forward for a lady to bring it up, though."

"Do I strike you as the sort who really cares what people think?"

Fargo chuckled. "No, not really."

Her hand tightened on his. "Go walk around the boat for half an hour. Then come to your cabin."

"Why the half hour?" Fargo asked as he tried not to frown in puzzlement.

Alexis laughed lightly. "A lady has to prepare for certain things. And while I don't mind admitting that I'm not very ladylike in some respects, in others I am."

"That's fine," Fargo said. "I'll be looking forward to it."

"So will I." Alexis drank the last of her wine. "I'm not hungry anymore. Not for food, anyway."

With the deliciously wicked image of her smile as she said that burning in his mind, Fargo stood up after she was gone. He went over to the bar and paused next to Cord Trahearne.

"Your sister is looking for you," he said.

Cord grunted and kept his eyes on the drink in his hand. "I'll go back to the cabin in a minute," he said. "As soon as I finish this drink."

"She just wants to help you keep out of trouble, Cord."

The young man didn't say anything, so Fargo left him

there. The alternative was to grab him by the shoulders and try to shake some sense into his stubborn head, and Fargo just wasn't in the mood to do that.

He went out on the texas deck, strolled along it and found the door to his cabin, then continued walking. The *Rockport* wasn't all that big. Fargo made the circuit of all three decks and wound up forward on the main deck, where the cargo was stacked. Night had fallen, so the men who had been there earlier playing cards were gone. Apparently, no one was around at all. Fargo wasn't surprised, though, when a quiet voice challenged him from the darkness as he approached the crates.

"Who's there?"

"Fargo," he said, recognizing the voice. "We met earlier, Major."

The rank was a guess, but evidently a good one, because Fargo heard a sharply indrawn breath of surprise. "How did you know?" the man asked as he stepped out from behind a stack of crates. He had his gun in his hand, but he lowered the weapon and pointed it toward the deck now that he knew who Fargo was. Angrily, he added, "Did MacGuinness tell you?"

"Nope," Fargo said. "I've just been around a lot of army officers before. Not your General Basswood, but plenty of others. If you know anything about me, you know I've worked with the army many times and never had any real trouble with them."

"Yes, I've heard all about the famous Trailsman," the man muttered as he holstered his gun. "MacGuinness thinks that we should ask you to help us."

"Chances are, I'd be agreeable to that."

"Unfortunately, involving a civilian is outside the scope of my orders. Whatever you think is going on here, Fargo, I have to ask you to ignore it and let us handle our own affairs."

"If that's what you want," Fargo said, matching the officer's cool, formal tone. "I'm not in the habit of sticking my nose into other people's business, especially when it's not wanted."

That wasn't always true, of course. But when he went against that policy, he nearly always wound up in some sort of ruckus—usually with gunplay involved.

"I'd be obliged, though, if you'd at least tell me your name," he went on. "We may not be working together, but we're not enemies."

"I suppose not." The man lowered his voice. "You were right about my rank. I'm Major Stuart Emory."

"Good to meet you, Major."

"Please, I'd rather you didn't call me that. No one on board but Captain MacGuinness and my men—and now you—know that I'm an army officer."

Fargo wouldn't have been so sure about that. It seemed to him that anybody with eyes in their head could tell that the man was an officer of some sort. But he said, "Sure, whatever you say, Emory. But if you need any help between here and Fort Benton, I'll be somewhere on board."

"I'll keep that in mind," Emory said, although his tone made it clear that he considered the chances of him asking Fargo for help were very remote.

Fargo had a pretty accurate clock in his head. He figured enough time had passed for him to head to his rendezvous with Alexis Rimbard. He said, "Good night," stopping himself before he added "Major."

Emory stepped back into the thick shadows between two stacks of crates. Fargo wondered if any of the troopers were hidden around the deck, or if the major was guarding the shipment alone. He hoped that Emory had more sense than that—but he wouldn't count on it.

When he reached the texas deck, he walked faster as he approached his cabin. He hadn't been in there yet, but he

76

ously, the young man had been close enough to overhear what the captain said.

Laurie went on. "He told me you were having dinner with a very beautiful woman, too. Why did you agree to have dinner with us if you already had plans with her?"

Fargo sat up. He forced a chuckle and said, "Out on the frontier, a fella eats when he gets the chance, because he never knows for sure when his next meal will be."

"I see. Who is she, Skye?"

Fargo felt a flash of annoyance. He didn't need Laurie getting jealous. If he had known what was going on, he wouldn't have been in this situation to start with. After telling Cord that a man had to be careful all the time on the frontier, he had gone and let his own guard down.

He swung his legs out of the bunk, stood up, felt around for his buckskins, and found a lucifer. He lit it with a snap of his thumbnail and held the flame to the wick of the cabin's single lamp, which was attached to the wall. As the yellow glow filled the room, he turned toward the bed and saw that Laurie was sitting up now, her long red hair loose around her shoulders and flowing down her back. Her creamy skin was lightly freckled, and Fargo could see most of it. He had to admit that she made a mighty appealing picture.

She had known what she was doing, too, and the fact that he had penetrated her with such ease told him that he hadn't stolen her innocence or anything like that. So he didn't have to feel guilty, just irritated at this unwanted complication.

"She's a gambler," he said. "Her name is Alexis Rimbard. She travels on this riverboat, and others that journey up and down the Missouri."

"I see. And did you have any plans with her other than dinner?"

Fargo wanted to tell her that was none of her damned business. He tightened his jaw to keep from saying it.

Then the door opened. Alexis must have been standing right outside, close enough to hear Laurie's question, because she regarded Fargo with a cool gaze and said, "Yes, Skye, tell me . . . what exactly *were* your plans for the evening?"

6

Standing there naked between two beautiful women was a mite disconcerting, even for a man of the world like Fargo. Laurie gasped and pulled the sheet up to cover herself, but Fargo didn't have that option.

So he mentally said the hell with it and just stood there unashamed. Telling the truth was generally the best option, so that's what he did now.

"You know what my plans were, Alexis. I was going to meet you here and take you to bed." He inclined his head toward the bunk. "By the way, this is Laurie Trahearne. Laurie, Alexis Rimbard."

"Yes, I figured as much, after you told me about having dinner with her," Laurie said, her voice cold with anger.

Alexis' smile was just as chilly. "I know you probably think pretty highly of yourself, Skye, but did you really believe you could rut with this little trollop and still have enough left to satisfy me?"

"Trollop!" Laurie cried. "Why, you—"

Fargo held up a hand to stop her. "This is all a misunderstanding," he said. "Laurie was here in my cabin waiting for me. When I came in, it was dark and I thought—"

He stopped short, realizing that what he was about to say wasn't going to sound right, but it was too late. "Oh!" Laurie said. "You thought I was *her*!"

"Ridiculous," Alexis said with a disdainful sniff. "You couldn't have mistaken that skinny little girl for me."

"I'm only skinny compared to you, you big cow!"

Fargo was ready to get between them if Alexis lost her temper and tried to attack Laurie, but instead Alexis just shook her head contemptuously and said, "Good night, Skye. It's a real shame you made such a *mistake*."

She turned and stalked back out the door, slamming it behind her. Fargo swung around toward Laurie and started to say, "I didn't mean for that to—"

"I know what you meant to happen," she said as she stood up and reached for her dress. Angrily, she jerked it on. "Good night . . . Mr. Fargo."

The door slammed behind her a second later.

Fargo stood there, not knowing whether to laugh or be angry. What had happened here was unfortunate in one respect—well, in several respects, he admitted—but it certainly hadn't been his fault. After a moment, he shook his head and laughed. Sometimes a fella just had to accept the fact that life was going to play tricks on him every now and then. It had certainly played one on him tonight.

With that thought, Fargo climbed contentedly back into the bunk, which was still warm from Laurie's body, and dropped off almost immediately into a deep, dreamless sleep.

The first part of the voyage, across Missouri to Westport Landing, just across the river from Kansas Territory, was easy. The river was deeper here, and although there were still snags to be avoided, an experienced captain such as F. X. MacGuinness could keep his vessel chugging along at a fairly fast pace.

At Westport Landing, the stream curved to the north, following the border between Nebraska Territory and Iowa. This part of the journey was still relatively free of any danger, as long as whoever was at the helm of the riverboat kept his eyes open and steered around any obstacles. Yankton, in Dakota Territory, was where the Missouri began angling more to the northwest. Yankton was also the last real settlement, although there were a number of military forts and trading posts scattered along the river between there and Fort Benton, which was the end of the line. Beyond that point the Big Muddy was no longer navigable.

Fargo knew better than to let the fast pace early on fool him. The farther north and west the *Rockport* traveled, the shallower and more treacherous the river would be. Sternwheelers had a very shallow draft and therefore didn't need much water. But even though the streambed might be hundreds of yards wide at places in Dakota Territory, the channel that held enough water to float the riverboat was much narrower, in some places almost as narrow as the vessel itself. The water everywhere except in the channel was only a few inches deep. Even the best captains had a difficult time making the run to Fort Benton without getting stuck several times on sandbars in the river. It could take an entire day to work a boat loose when it found itself in that predicament. A journey all the way from Saint Louis to Fort Benton took at least six weeks. Unexpected delays could push the time up to more than two months.

So Fargo didn't get excited when the *Rockport* put Westport Landing behind it less than a week into the voyage. He knew that the trip would get a lot tougher.

Laurie had been cool toward him for several days after the incident in Fargo's cabin the first night out of Saint Louis. Cord didn't seem to like him much to start with. Only Denny was still friendly toward him.

Gradually, Laurie began to warm up to him again. As she explained one morning when she invited Fargo to join her for breakfast, "You *did* risk your life to help us out, back there in Saint Louis." She lowered her voice. "And you sure didn't know I was going to be there in your cabin." Cord and Denny weren't up yet, she had said when Fargo sat down with her, but even so she wanted to be discreet about what had happened between them, he thought.

"Things might have been different if I had known," Fargo admitted.

"Oh?" She leaned closer to him. "What would you have done? Made me leave?"

Fargo smiled. "I didn't say that. I'm not sure what I would have done." He grew more serious. "A woman deserves to have a fella's complete attention when he's with her, though. Otherwise it's just not fair."

"Are you saying you could have . . . done better?"

"Maybe we'll find out . . . one of these days."

The flush that comment brought to her face made her even prettier, Fargo thought. He detected interest in her eyes. He wasn't going to try to rush her into anything, though. Whether by accident or design, they had shared a special moment, but he didn't want to pressure her into repeating it.

Alexis, on the other hand, made it clear that he had missed his chance with her. During the one conversation of substance he'd had with her since that night, she had told him that she had run into Captain MacGuinness again on her way to his cabin, and he had talked to her for so long she'd been late getting there. That was pure bad luck, but Alexis wasn't going to go against it. They weren't meant to be together, she had told Fargo, and she knew better than to tempt fate. Reluctantly, he had accepted that decision.

So he didn't get to enjoy Alexis' company, and for the moment, at least, the same was true of Laurie. But there were worse things than taking a leisurely boat ride up the Missouri River. The weather was nice, and although the country grew flatter and uglier the farther north and west they went, Fargo expected that. He had traveled through this region many times.

They left Yankton behind and followed the river deeper into Dakota Territory. So far Cord had behaved himself and not tried to trick any members of the *Rockport*'s crew into fighting Denny. Likewise, no one had bothered the cargo that Major Stuart Emory and his men were on board to protect. Fargo began to wonder about that. Fort Stevenson was the last actual military outpost. Although Fort Union and Fort Benton still lay ahead, despite their names they were settlements that had grown up around trading posts from the old fur trapping days. Fargo had expected Emory and his men to get off the boat at one of those army posts, but they were still aboard. Maybe his hunch about why they were heading upriver was wrong.

The days passed and continued to turn into weeks. Fort Union fell behind. In another week, maybe less if they were lucky, they would be in Fort Benton.

Fargo was in his cabin that evening when a soft knock sounded on the door. He had already stripped down to his waist, getting ready to turn in. He slid the Colt from its holster, where it lay on a chair with the coiled shell belt, and went to the door. When he opened it, he found Laurie standing there.

"Something wrong?" he asked. "Has Cord finally gotten up to some sort of mischief again?"

She shook her head. "No, he and Denny are already asleep. I just wanted to see you again, Skye."

For a while after that first night, she had called him "Mr. Fargo," but that had worn off as she got over being mad and acted friendlier toward him again. With his customary courtesy, he moved back and held out a hand to invite her into the cabin.

She stepped inside. Fargo closed the door and turned to face her. He put the gun back in its holster.

"I'm sorry," she said. "I realize that you weren't to blame for what happened that night. I haven't come right out and said that, and I think I ought to before we get to Fort Benton. You've been so kind to us. I don't want any hard feelings between us."

"There are none on my part," Fargo told her honestly.

"I mean . . ." She blushed prettily. "What happened was good. Really good."

"It was," Fargo agreed.

"And I was just thinking . . ."

She looked down at the floor. Fargo put his hand under her chin and tilted her head up again so that he could look into her lovely green eyes.

"Thinking that maybe we ought to do it again?" he asked softly.

"Oh, my, yes!" she said as she came forward into his arms.

Fargo kissed her. Somehow, she tasted even better with the lamp burning than she had in the darkness. He supposed that was because this time, he *knew* he was kissing Laurie Trahearne. There was no confusion, no mistaken identity this time. He was kissing Laurie, she was kissing him, and they both knew they wanted each other.

Her hands played over his muscular chest. "Make love to me, Skye," she whispered when her lips drew back from his.

"I'd be mighty glad to," he told her. His hands went around her to the buttons on the back of her dress. When he had them undone, he drew the garment down over her shoulders and arms and pushed it to her waist, baring her firm, lightly freckled breasts with their pale pink nipples. He bent and drew the nipple on her left breast into his mouth, running his tongue around it as it hardened. She made a soft noise of passion in her throat.

Fargo tongued and sucked both breasts, then pushed Laurie's dress the rest of the way to the floor. She wore nothing underneath it, so she was ready for him when he picked her up and carried her to the bunk. As he placed her on her back, her legs parted as if by instinct, drawing him to the already wet opening at the base of the triangle of red hair. Fargo knelt and pressed his mouth to her sex, running the tip of his tongue between the folds. They hadn't gotten to do this the first time, and he looked forward to the pleasure he intended to give her.

Within minutes, his fingers and tongue brought her to climax. Then, while she was still catching her breath, he mounted her and filled her with his hard shaft. She clutched at him and bucked her hips up to meet his powerful thrusts. Fargo sent her climbing the heights she had just scaled, and after a few minutes, they toppled over the peak together.

Spent, Fargo rolled off her and lay beside her on the bunk, which was narrow enough so that their bodies were pressed together for their full length. Neither of them minded that. Laurie closed a hand around his softening member and squeezed it affectionately.

"I've never known a man like you, Skye," she said. "I'm not sure there are any more like you."

He chuckled. "Are you saying they broke the mold when they made me?"

"Don't get too much of a swelled head," she said with a laugh. "I haven't tried all the men on the frontier yet."

"Is that what you have in mind?"

"You never know," she said.

Fargo slid an arm around her, drew her close to him. She buried her face against his shoulder.

"I'd never try any other man," she whispered, "if I thought I could hold you, Skye Fargo."

"I've never been one to stay in the same place for long," he told her gently. He didn't want to hurt her, but he wasn't going to lie to her, either.

"I know that. You're the Trailsman. You always have to find new trails. Once we get to Fort Benton, if my father's there . . . I know you'll probably ride on."

Fargo didn't say anything. He just stroked her hair.

"And that's all right," Laurie went on. "We've had our time together. I'm just sorry I was so stiff-necked and stubborn that I wasted so much of it."

"It hasn't been wasted," Fargo told her. "It's been a good trip. And there aren't a whole lot of women out here yet, so I'm sure you'll meet some nice fella and settle down. You'll have your pick of plenty of men."

"Not really. My pick is right here."

She sounded sleepy as she said it, and Fargo wouldn't have been surprised if she had dozed off. It would have been all right with him, too.

But instead she sat up a moment later and said, "I have to go. I don't want Denny to wake up and find that I'm not there. He'd get confused and scared."

"He's a mighty lucky young man to have a sister who watches out for him like you do."

"Most people wouldn't consider Denny lucky at all," Laurie said as she swung her legs out of the bunk and reached for her dress on the floor. "I mean, the way he is . . . simpleminded and all . . ."

Fargo sat up. "His brain may not work as well as some, but from what I've seen of him, his heart works better than most people's do."

Laurie leaned over and kissed Fargo. "That's such a sweet thing to say."

Then he felt pure shock go through him as she picked up the gown, reached into its folds, and turned back around with a double-barreled derringer in her hand.

"I'm sorry, Skye," she said as she pointed the weapon at his face from a distance of no more than a foot. "I lied. I'm not unarmed. But please don't move, or I'll be forced to kill you, and under the circumstances, I really don't want to."

Fargo didn't move, despite the surprise he felt. Alexis was standing close enough to him he might have been able to knock the derringer aside before she could fire. But she had eared back both hammers as she turned, and her finger hovered over the triggers. If she managed to fire before he could bat the barrels out of line, the slugs would blow a big, fatal hole in his head.

"What the hell is this?" he asked. "Is this your idea of getting back at me for what happened that first night? Make love to me and then kill me?"

"Not at all. I'm trying to keep you from dying. If you just sit right there and don't move, maybe you'll live through this."

Fargo was about to ask her what she was talking about, but before he could do so, shots blasted out, somewhere else on the riverboat. The *Rockport* tied up every night, because it was too dangerous to try to navigate the Missouri River in the darkness. With the engine off, quiet usually reigned, but tonight gunfire, shouted curses, and cries of pain shattered that peace.

"What the hell have you done?" Fargo grated.

"Taken the first step toward being rich," Alexis said. "Money may not matter all that much to you, Skye, but it does to everybody else. And I'm finally going to have plenty of—"

Running footsteps suddenly pounded on the deck right outside the cabin door. A shot roared. Instinct made Alexis jerk her head in that direction.

Fargo had been waiting for something like that. He exploded off the bunk, sweeping his left hand up and hitting Alexis' right wrist. That knocked the derringer to the side. She jerked the triggers anyway, firing both barrels. Even though the derringer was small, at such close range the sound of the shots was loud enough to slam into Fargo's ear almost like a fist. He ignored the discomfort and grabbed Alexis.

Not surprisingly, she fought back. She slashed at Fargo's head with the empty gun, and as he ducked under the blow, she tried to bring her knee up into his groin. Since he was naked, the vicious blow might have put him out of the fight and left him curled up on the floor in a ball of agony if it had connected. As it was, he twisted aside just in time to take her knee on his thigh. He swung her around, plucked the gun out of her hand, and shoved her into the bunk.

"Stay there, damn it!" he said. Then he lunged for his buckskins and his Colt. Shots were still going off elsewhere on the boat. He had to get out there and find out what was going on.

Fear for Laurie, Denny, and yes, even Cord formed a cold ball in the pit of his stomach. Thoughts flashed through his mind as he yanked his trousers on and jerked the .44 from its holster. Outlaws had finally attacked the riverboat, he told himself, going after whatever it was Major Emory and the rest of the soldiers had been guarding.

And Alexis had known the attack was going to take place. She hadn't come here to his cabin tonight to make amends for what had happened in the past. She had come to distract him and then get the drop on him when the right moment came.

She was part of the gang. That was the only conclusion Fargo could draw.

It had taken him only a split second to come to that conclusion once the shooting started. Now he didn't know what he could do to stop the outlaws from taking over the boat, but he wasn't going to let them get away with it without a fight.

As he stepped toward the door, however, it flew open. Fargo brought the Colt up, then froze with his finger on the trigger as he recognized Major Emory. The army officer had a gun in his hand and a bloody scratch on his cheek that looked like a bullet had grazed him, but he seemed to be all right other than that. Fargo felt a surge of hope that the troops and the boat crew had been able to fight off the attack.

"Major," he began, "what happ—"

"Stu, no!" Alexis screamed. "Don't!"

In that shaved instant of time, Fargo's gun snapped up and bucked against his palm as he triggered a shot. Instinct had done it, a warning bell that had gone off in his mind as soon as Alexis cried out. Emory was in on it, too, Fargo knew in that moment.

As fast as Fargo's reaction was, Emory still managed to fire first. Smoke and flame geysered from the muzzle of his gun. Fargo felt something crash against his head. It sent him stumbling backward even as he saw Emory double over in pain. Fargo felt himself falling but couldn't catch his balance. He crashed to the floor. The Colt slipped out of his fingers.

Alexis was there to kick it away before he could get his hand on it again. She loomed over him, breasts heaving, as naked as some primitive warrior princess. Blackness had begun to close in from the edges of Fargo's vision, like thick curtains, but he could still see her clearly.

"You should have listened to me, Skye," she said as she bent to pick up his Colt. "He might not have shot you if he hadn't seen you with a gun in your hand."

Something hot and wet slid down Fargo's face. Blood. Had to be. It gave a crimson tinge to that encroaching blackness. He tried to get his muscles to work, to lift him from the floor, but they ignored the urgent messages his brain sent to them.

"I'm sorry," Alexis whispered.

Fargo wanted to tell her to go to hell and take her apology with her. But then those black curtains closed all the way, and she was gone.

So was he.

7

Fargo was a little surprised when he woke up. He figured that Alexis would have put a bullet in his brain after he passed out.

Maybe she had, judging by the agony that pounded through his skull. Maybe he was dead. But that couldn't be, because folks who were dead didn't hurt this bad.

How do you know that? he asked himself. It wasn't like anybody could tell him that was true.

Then he shifted slightly and heard a faint rustling sound. He recognized it as the noise a cornhusk mattress made whenever someone lying on it moved around. He felt a sheet underneath him and knew he was in a bunk.

So he wasn't dead after all. He just hurt so much he almost wished he were.

Almost—but not quite. Fargo intended to cling to life just as long as he possibly could, no matter how painful it might be.

He heard someone groan and realized a second later it was him. A man's voice said, "He's waking up."

"Fargo?" That voice belonged to another man and was vaguely familiar. "Fargo, can you hear me?"

Captain somebody-or-other . . . MacGuinness, that was it. Captain F. X. MacGuinness, master of the stern-wheeler *Rockport*, the boat that had been carrying Fargo to Fort Benton along with Laurie Trahearne and her brothers, and Alexis Rimbard—

Fargo groaned again and forced his eyes open as the rest of the memories came flooding back into his aching brain. He recalled how both Laurie and Alexis had come to his cabin to make love, and how Alexis had double-crossed him and pulled that derringer afterward. Then Major Emory had come in, that traitorous bastard, and Fargo had exchanged shots with him.

Captain MacGuinness' round, florid face, dark against the white goatee, loomed over him. "Can you hear me, Fargo?"

"I hear you," Fargo said. He tried to sit up, but the room spun crazily around him. He slumped back down on the bunk and lifted a hand to his head. His fingers touched cloth. He realized that somebody had tied a bandage around his head.

"Take it easy," MacGuinness cautioned. "You're not hurt bad, but a bullet grazed your head. A hard knock like that will leave a man pretty addled."

"I remember what happened," Fargo said. "Somebody help me up."

MacGuinness nodded to another man, who grasped Fargo's arm and steadied him. Fargo sat up on the bunk and put a hand against the wall to brace himself until the room settled down, which it did after a moment. Fargo looked around and saw that MacGuinness and two other men were crowded into the cabin. He recognized the other men as members of the riverboat's crew.

The captain had a bloody bandage tied around his left shoulder, and a makeshift sling supported that arm. His face was bruised and scratched, as though he had taken a beating. Crimson-stained bandages testified that the other men had been injured in the fighting, too, but they didn't seem badly hurt.

"Where's Emory?" Fargo rasped.

"Gone," MacGuinness replied with a bitter edge in his

voice. "He left with those damned pirates who attacked the boat."

"He was wounded . . . we traded shots, and I know I hit him . . ."

"That's right," MacGuinness said. "He had help getting off the boat. I don't know how badly he was hurt. I had problems of my own just then." He gestured with his right hand toward his wounded left shoulder.

"How bad are you hit?" Fargo asked.

"I reckon I'll live. The bullet seems to have missed the bone. It carved out a chunk of meat and I lost quite a bit of blood. Mainly, though, I'm just mad. That son of a bitch fooled me good and proper."

"You mean Emory?"

MacGuinness snorted. "Who else? Came aboard and told me he had a shipment of rifles bound for a new fort being built west of Fort Benton, at the foot of the Rockies. And I believed him, fool that I am."

"It was a plausible story," Fargo said. "What was in the cargo, if it wasn't rifles?"

"I don't know. Once they took over the boat, they unloaded the crates, but I never saw what was inside them."

"What about the other men in the guard detail?"

"Dead," MacGuinness replied grimly. "Emory made sure they all died first."

"Start from the beginning. Tell me what happened."

"Are you sure you're up to it? Maybe you should get some rest."

Fargo didn't figure he'd be getting much rest anytime soon. "Just tell me," he said.

"Emory must have knifed the man who was on watch in the pilothouse. We found him dead with a stab wound in his back. That let the gang of pirates he was working with get onto the boat before any of the rest of us knew they were here. There were about a dozen of them, best I could tell from what I saw and from talking to the crew. Like I told you, the first thing they did was gun down those troopers, except for the sergeant. I reckon he was in on it with Emory." Wearily, MacGuinness scrubbed his right hand over his face. "Then they came after the crew. I rang the alarm bell when the shooting started, but of course, it was too late by then. The bastards were already all over my boat."

"How did you survive the fight?" Fargo asked.

"Half a dozen of us managed to get into the pilothouse and forted up there. The only way to get there is up one narrow set of stairs, so they knew better than to rush us. We'd have killed too many of them. So some of them were content to keep us pinned down while the rest carried that cargo ashore. I think they had wagons waiting there, but I'm not sure about that."

Fargo figured the captain was right. This act of river piracy had been well planned, so almost certainly the outlaws would have had wagons to carry off their loot.

"We tried to take some potshots at them," MacGuinness went on, "but they shot the pilothouse so full of holes about all we could do was keep our heads down and pray we wouldn't get ventilated, too. I saw the sergeant helping Emory off the boat. And then"—the captain's voice caught—"and then Alexis left with them, too."

Fargo nodded. "I was with her when Emory shot me. I knew she was part of it."

"That girl was almost like my own daughter!" MacGuinness burst out. "I never dreamed she was so treacherous!"

"Maybe she wasn't, starting out," Fargo said. "Maybe Emory came to her with the plan, and she just couldn't say no to the chance to be rich, however they intend to go about that."

"A shipment of army rifles would be worth quite a bit," MacGuinness said.

Fargo frowned. "Enough for an officer to throw away his career and risk his life?" He shook his head. "There's something else going on here, Captain. I just don't know what it is yet."

"Yet?" MacGuinness repeated.

"I'm going after them," Fargo said.

The captain looked at him for a moment, then nodded. "I should have figured as much. You're the Trailsman, after all."

"That's not it. I just don't want them getting away with whatever it is they've got in mind."

MacGuinness rubbed his jaw and grimaced. "You haven't heard all of it yet, Fargo, and this may be the worst to you. They took Miss Trahearne with them."

Shock stiffened Fargo's muscles. "Laurie?"

"Aye. I suppose they wanted a hostage, in case anybody came after them."

Fargo had wondered about Laurie's safety and had been about to ask MacGuinness about her when the captain broke the news that she had been carried off by the outlaws. "What about her brothers?"

"They're all right," MacGuinness said. "Several of the passengers who tried to put up a fight were killed, but most of them weren't harmed."

Fargo looked around and saw that he was still in his own cabin. His clothes and gear were there. He stood up, again bracing a hand against the wall when dizziness overtook him for a moment. "What about my horse?" he asked.

"Still there at the stern. Nobody bothered him, as far as I know."

Fargo nodded in relief. It would have been impossible for him to pursue the outlaws without the Ovaro.

He reached for his buckskin shirt. "I'll need a few supplies to take with me," he said.

"You're going alone?"

"That's right."

"Even if you manage to catch up to them, what can one man do against odds like that?"

"I don't know yet, but I have to try. Maybe I can get Miss Trahearne away from them, anyway."

"Or get the both of you killed."

"That's a chance I'll have to take," Fargo said.

"You'd best wait until morning. You can't track those scoundrels in the dark."

Fargo wasn't so sure about that. If there was enough moonlight, he might be able to follow the outlaws' tracks.

"And you'd have a little more time to recover from that knock on the head that way," MacGuinness continued. "It's not going to do Miss Trahearne any good if you pass out once you're away from the boat."

The captain might have a point there, Fargo thought as he finished buckling on his gun belt. He had suffered head wounds before and knew they could be tricky things. By morning, he would have a better idea of just how badly he was hurt.

"All right," he said as he eased on his hat, being careful not to dislodge the bandage around his head, "but first thing in the morning, I'm riding out."

"I'll not try to stop you," MacGuinness said. "I want justice to catch up to those bastards just as much as you do."

Fargo nodded. "Right now I want to talk to Laurie's brothers."

As they left the cabin and started toward the one shared by the Trahearnes, he went on, "I'm surprised those river pirates didn't try to kill everyone on board and burn the boat, so they wouldn't be leaving any witnesses behind."

"Oh, they tried to set fire to the boat," MacGuinness

said. "One fella got a torch lit, but before he could toss it into what was left of the cargo, one of my men shot him and knocked him into the water. Then the big bastard who was in charge yelled for the rest of them to forget it and come on. I reckon he knew we couldn't follow them, and he didn't want to risk losing any more men."

"Wait a minute," Fargo said with a frown. "Emory wasn't the leader of the gang?"

MacGuinness shook his head. "No, that was a varmint in what looked like a buffalo coat. Great big fella. He kept roaring orders, so I know he was in charge."

So Emory and Alexis had been working together, Fargo thought, and now this unknown desperado was linked to them somehow. Had Emory come to Alexis with the plan to steal whatever that mysterious cargo was, and she had put him in touch with the boss outlaw? That seemed reasonable to Fargo.

"When Emory came on board, he told you he was working for some general called Basswood, didn't he?"

"That's right. You think this General Basswood even really exists?"

"Probably. Emory couldn't have gotten those troopers to go along with him unless there was at least a little bit of truth to the story." Fargo paused at the railing to frown in thought. "Somehow, Emory faked all the orders he needed to get that cargo loaded on the boat and bring a detail of guards with him. The soldiers went along with him because they thought they were doing what they were supposed to do. But I'll bet Emory's superiors never knew a thing about it until it was too late."

"You're probably right," MacGuinness agreed. "Emory duped everybody and delivered that cargo to the outlaws. But he got a bullet for his trouble."

"We don't know how bad he was hit," Fargo pointed out. "He might pull through."

As he wondered about that, he wondered why Alexis had spared his life, as well. Head wounds were messy as hell; there had been blood all over the cabin floor where Fargo had been lying before MacGuinness and the other men found him and patched him up. Alexis might have been convinced that he was dying anyway, and she just hadn't taken the time to finish him off.

Or maybe what they had shared just before all hell broke loose had prompted her not to kill him. Fargo considered that sort of unlikely, since she had been willing to cast her lot with a traitor—Emory—and a bunch of outlaws, but he couldn't rule it out entirely.

Not that it mattered. Either way, he still intended to see that she faced justice for what she had done.

When they reached the Trahearnes' cabin, Fargo rapped on the door. Cord jerked it open instantly. "Mr. Fargo!" he exclaimed. "You're alive. We didn't know."

Denny's massive form loomed up behind his brother. "It's Mr. Fargo?" he asked. "Does he have Laurie with him?"

"No, I told you, Denny, those bad men took her with them." Cord turned back to Fargo and asked, "You *don't* have her, do you?"

Fargo shook his head. "I'm afraid not."

Cord closed his eyes and rubbed his temples. "For a second there, I hoped that maybe . . . But never mind. I'm glad to see that you're all right."

Fargo wouldn't have expected such concern from Cord. Evidently what had happened had shaken the youngster's cocky demeanor.

"Tell me what happened."

"There was a lot of shooting," Denny said. "Shooting, and people yelling. It scared me."

"We didn't know what was going on," Cord said. "We were all asleep, and then, like Denny said, we heard a bunch of shooting. People were running around on deck. Laurie said she had to make sure you were all right. She rushed out before Denny or I could stop her."

"You let her go?" Fargo asked with a frown.

"I told you, she rushed out because she was worried about you." Cord's tone was a little accusatory. "What was I supposed to do? Drag Denny out in the middle of a gun battle? I couldn't leave him here by himself. Anyway, even if I'd tried to do that, he would have followed me."

Cord was probably right about that, Fargo thought. And Denny would have made a big target for those outlaws if he'd been on deck.

"I knew she was going to your cabin," Cord went on. "I hoped she'd make it there all right, and then you would take care of her." He gestured toward the bloodstained bandage on Fargo's head. "Looks like you weren't in any shape to do that."

"I got creased by a slug," Fargo said, his voice curt. He didn't owe Cord any explanations. "Was that the last you saw of her?"

Cord shook his head. "No. When the shooting died down some, I risked going out to look for her. Some of the men who attacked the boat were carrying cargo ashore. That lady gambler I've seen in the salon, Miss Rimbard, I think her name is, she was with them . . . and she had Laurie with her. She was waving a gun around and giving orders, and then . . ." Cord hesitated as if he couldn't bring himself to go on. But after a second he continued, "Then this really big man who acted like he was the boss of the whole bunch came over and grabbed Laurie. He dragged her away. The Rimbard woman went with them."

So Alexis was the one behind Laurie's kidnapping, Fargo thought. Had she done it out of spite, because she knew there was something between Laurie and Fargo? Or had it simply been a matter of expediency, taking a hostage in case they were pursued?

Either way, that was one more thing Alexis had to answer for.

"Don't worry," Fargo said. "I'm going after them, and I'll bring Laurie back to you."

"We're coming with you," Cord said instantly.

"We'll help you find Laurie," Denny put in.

Fargo shook his head. "Sorry," he said, making his voice firm enough they would understand that he wasn't going to argue about it. "That's impossible. There are no horses for you, and you'd never catch up to those bastards on foot. You'd just slow me down."

"There were a dozen of them, maybe more," Cord protested. "You won't stand a chance against them by yourself."

"I don't reckon a couple of farm boys from Ohio would be much help." Fargo wasn't trying to insult them, but he wasn't going to pull any punches, either.

Cord's face flushed with anger. "I can handle a gun," he said, "and you've seen Denny fight. We can take care of ourselves. We won't slow you down, and we won't be a burden."

"Denny's as good in a rough-and-tumble brawl as anybody I've ever seen," Fargo admitted, "but that doesn't mean anything in a gunfight. Anyway, *there are no horses except my Ovaro*."

That was one obstacle the Trahearne brothers couldn't overcome. Cord sighed and said, "It's not fair."

"There's plenty in life that isn't," Fargo said. "But you have my word, I'll do everything in my power to bring Laurie back to you, safe and sound."

"I hope you do, Mr. Fargo," Denny said. "I really miss her already. If I never see her again, I . . . I'll . . ." His face contorted, and he started to cry.

Cord tried to comfort his brother. He glanced back over his shoulder at Fargo and said, "There's one more thing you can do . . . Kill every one of those sons of bitches."

"Do my best," Fargo said.

It had been fairly late when the river pirates attacked, and Fargo had been out for a while after that, so it wasn't too many hours until dawn. Fargo used that time to gather some supplies from the *Rockport*'s kitchen and check on the Ovaro.

"I know you're ready to get out and hit the trail again, big fella," he told the stallion. "You're going to get your chance pretty soon now."

The fact that the outlaws were using wagons to transport the stolen cargo meant that they couldn't move too fast. Even with a night's lead, Fargo was confident that he could catch up to them without too much trouble. Then it would be time to figure out how one man could take on a dozen or more brutal killers and have any chance of coming out on top.

A light burned in the pilothouse. Fargo climbed up there. Before he reached the door, it opened and Captain MacGuinness peered out, a revolver in his good hand.

"Oh, it's you, Fargo," he said. "I heard somebody coming. I didn't think those pirates would have come back tonight, but I couldn't be sure. What can I do for you?"

"The cook gave me some salt pork and flour, sugar, and coffee," Fargo said. "I'm hoping you've got a rifle you can spare. I left my Henry back in Saint Louis."

"Come on in." MacGuinness tucked the pistol behind his belt as Fargo entered the pilothouse. "As a matter of fact, I've got an old Sharps I sometimes use to take a few shots at buffalo when we come across a herd grazing on the banks. Ever use one before?"

Fargo grinned. "A time or two," he said dryly. He had carried a Sharps for years before he'd starting using the Henry. He still liked the Sharps and considered it a solid, dependable weapon with incredible range and stopping power. The biggest advantage the Henry had over it was that the Henry was a fifteen-shot repeater.

MacGuinness opened a cabinet and took out a Sharps carbine. He held it out to Fargo and said, "You're welcome to it, as long as you use it to shoot some of those bastards."

Fargo took the Sharps and repeated the promise he had made to Cord Trahearne. "I'll do my best."

"There's a box of shells here, too." MacGuinness handed them over.

"Much obliged." Fargo felt better now that he had the Sharps. He was fully armed again for the first time since leaving Saint Louis.

The pain in his head had receded to a dull ache. His vision was all right, as far as he could tell. He said to MacGuinness, "There's one more favor you can do for me, Captain."

"Anything, as long as you're going after those outlaws."

"Look at my eyes," Fargo said.

MacGuinness frowned in puzzlement. "What about 'em?"

"Is the pupil the same size in each eye?"

MacGuinness studied Fargo's eyes, looking back and forth between them for a moment, then said, "Yeah, as far as I can tell, they are. Why?"

"I once ran into a fella who'd had some medical training back east. He told me that was one way you could tell if somebody's brain was hurt from a wallop on the head. One pupil will be bigger than the other, and if it is, it's dangerous for them to be up and around, doing much."

"What would you have done if that's the way your eyes were?"

Fargo grunted. "Probably risked it and gone after those outlaws anyway. I can't ignore what they've done, or the danger that Miss Trahearne is in."

MacGuinness shook his head. "If there was any way to do it, I'd go with you, Fargo, and I reckon the whole crew would, too. But like you told those Trahearne boys, we'd never catch up to them on foot. Best I can do is take the old *Rockport* on to Fort Benton and spread the word about what happened. Might be some fellas there who could come to help you. They'd have to start trailing you from right here, though, because by then we won't have any way of knowing where you are."

"It's still a good idea," Fargo said. "I'll blaze a trail."

Fargo knew that some of the old-time mountain men were still around this region. If even a few of them came after him to lend a hand, that would go a long way toward evening up the odds.

The sky was beginning to turn gray in the east with the approach of dawn. Fargo planned to take up the trail at first light. He thanked MacGuinness again for the loan of the Sharps, then went back down to the kitchen to get an early breakfast from the cook. He wasn't really very hungry, but he knew it would be smart to go ahead and eat before he left.

He was finishing up a tin cup of coffee—after promising the cook that, yes, he would do his best to kill the bastards who had raided the boat—when one of the surviving crew members hurried into the kitchen and said, "Mr. Fargo, Cap'n MacGuinness wanted me to tell you that there are three riders comin' along the south bank."

Fargo drained the last of the coffee and set the cup down. "Indians?" he asked.

"No, sir. White men."

Fargo nodded and followed the crewman out of the kitchen onto the main deck. He carried the Sharps in his left hand. Along this stretch of the river, the banks rose ten or fifteen feet on either side of the broad, muddy, twisting streambed but sloped gently enough to allow easy access to the river. The sun wasn't quite up yet, but the sky was light enough for Fargo to see the silhouettes of the three riders as they came closer to the boat.

They were white men, all right. With the rising sun behind them, Fargo couldn't make out many details, but he could tell from the hats the men wore and the fact they rode saddled horses that they weren't Indians.

MacGuinness hurried down from the pilothouse, where he must have spotted the riders. "Do you think some of those river pirates have come back?" he asked Fargo.

"If they belonged to that bunch, it's not likely they'd ride up right out in the open like that," Fargo said. "Pass the word among your men to be ready for trouble, though, just in case."

MacGuinness nodded and hurried off. Fargo walked up to the bow, where the cargo that hadn't been stolen was still stacked around. He set the Sharps on a crate and put his right foot up on the low rail that ran around the edge of the deck.

The three men rode down to the river's edge and reined in. About fifteen feet separated them from Fargo. "Hello, the boat!" one of them called. "This be the *Rockport*?"

"It is," Fargo replied. "What can I do for you?"

Another of the strangers laughed. "You can't be the captain, not in them buckskins."

"I'm not the captain," Fargo said, "but it's me you're talking to."

That brought glares from all three men. They were big, hard-faced hombres, each with several weeks' growth of beard. They had rifles across their saddles and six-guns on their hips. Something about them seemed familiar to Fargo, but he was fairly sure he had never seen any of them before.

The first man who had spoken edged his horse a step ahead of the others and said, "Actually, I got an idea that you're the man we're lookin' for. We was told he was a big gent in buckskins, answers to the name of Skye Fargo."

"That's me," Fargo said with a nod.

"Well, sir, my name is Joseph, and these here are my brothers Edgar and Colston. Those names mean anything to you?"

Fargo shook his head. "I'm afraid not."

"Maybe our last name does. It's Mullaney. You killed our brother, you son of a bitch, and now we aim to kill you!"

With that, all three of them jerked their rifles to their shoulders.

8

The grudge the Mullaney brothers had nursed all the way from Saint Louis had made them stupid. The smart thing to do would have been to ride up, make sure of who Fargo was, and then start blazing away at him without announcing their intentions. But Joseph Mullaney had been so intent on Fargo knowing who they were and why they were trying to kill him, that he had given Fargo an extra split second to act.

With the Trailsman, that split second was fatal.

The Colt leaped into Fargo's hand so swiftly it was just a blur of speed. The revolver bucked and roared before Joseph's rifle ever had a chance to come to bear on Fargo. Joseph jerked back in the saddle as the .44 caliber slug punched into his forehead and bored on into his brain. The rifle kept rising and Joseph's finger clenched involuntarily on the trigger as he died, but by that time the barrel was angled upward and the shot went harmlessly into the sky.

The other two Mullaney brothers managed to fire their rifles. Fargo had already dropped into a crouch at the edge of the deck before the heavy boom of his first shot even echoed off the riverbanks. One of the slugs aimed at him chewed into a crate a couple of feet to his left. The other whipped past his ear and whined on across the river. He triggered again as he shifted his aim to the brother who had been to Joseph's left. He didn't know if that was Edgar or Colston and didn't give a damn. He planned to kill all three of the men who had ridden hundreds of miles up the Big Muddy just to avenge their bloodthirsty brute of a brother.

The second Mullaney dropped his rifle and sagged in the saddle as Fargo's bullet ripped through his body. His horse, spooked by the shooting, capered to the side, and the wounded man pitched off. His foot hung in the stirrup, though, and as the horse bolted and started dragging him along the edge of the river, the man screamed.

Fargo rolled to the right as another slug knocked splinters from the deck only inches away. The remaining Mullaney brother screamed curses at him and kept firing. The man had a Henry, and from the way he was acting, he intended to empty it. Fargo came to a stop behind a crate, and as bullets thudded into it, he hoped there wasn't any blasting powder or anything like that in it.

Fargo yanked off his hat, tossed it one way to get the man's attention, then went the other way in a sprawling dive that carried him back out into the open. Lying on his side, he lifted the Colt and thumbed off two fast shots. The man dropped his rifle and clutched at his throat as at least one of Fargo's bullets ripped the flesh open. Blood spouted between the wounded man's fingers in a crimson arc. He swayed in the saddle for a second, then toppled sideways and crashed to the ground.

The whole fight had taken maybe fifteen seconds. All three of the Mullaney brothers were down, and their horses milled around the edge of the river. The man whose foot had caught in the stirrup had finally slipped free. He lay facedown in the shallow water.

Fargo kept the Colt pointed toward the three men as he climbed to his feet. He still had one round left in the cylinder, and he intended to use it if any of them moved. The Sharps was within reach, too.

"Good Lord!" MacGuinness called down from the texas deck. "I was going to help you, Fargo, but the fight was over too damn fast!"

"If you have to kill a man, it's best to do it as quickly as you can," Fargo said. "The longer he stays alive, the better the chance he'll kill you."

"Who were they?"

"Brothers of a man I had to shoot back in Saint Louis."

"And they followed you all this way?" MacGuinness sounded like he could hardly believe it.

"Hate will keep a man going for a long time."

Satisfied that none of the Mullaney brothers were going to move again, Fargo reloaded the Colt and pouched the iron. He picked up his hat and the Sharps and walked across the gangplank that had been put in place when the riverboat tied up here the night before.

Now that the shooting was over, the passengers were starting to come out to see what had happened. Quite a few people were on deck by the time Fargo finished checking the bodies. All three men were dead, just as he had thought. He approached the horses slowly, speaking quietly to them in order to soothe their gunfire-frazzled nerves, and gathered their reins in his free hand. He led the animals back toward the boat. They nickered at the Ovaro.

The sun was up now, peeking over the eastern horizon. Fargo didn't want to burn any more daylight than he had to, so he waved the Sharps toward the corpses and called to MacGuinness, "You reckon you can see to burying these fellas?"

"Don't worry. We'll take care of it," MacGuinness assured him. "Although it would be easier to leave them for the wolves." The captain heaved a sigh. "Don't reckon we can do that, though. I wouldn't feel right about it."

"Neither would I," Fargo said. He tied the horses to a scrubby bush and came back aboard.

Cord and Denny were waiting for him at the end of the gangplank. "We're coming with you," Cord said as soon as Fargo stepped on deck.

"I told you—"

"You said there were no horses," Cord interrupted. "Now there are. There's even an extra one for Laurie."

He pointed at the mounts the Mullaney brothers had ridden.

Fargo shook his head. "You'd still hold me back. And I'd have to worry about whether or not you two got killed, instead of concentrating on rescuing Laurie."

"I told you we can take care of ourselves," Cord insisted. "Both of us can ride. Hell, if we slow you down, there wouldn't be anything stopping you from riding off and leaving us."

"I'd do it, too, if I had to," Fargo warned.

"Damn right you would. That's our sister's life that's at stake."

Fargo rubbed his bearded jaw and frowned. "What about guns? That little pistol of yours won't be much good in a real fight."

Cord pointed again, this time at the dead men. "There are plenty of guns and ammunition right there."

The youngster had a point. Fargo already had his eye on the Henry rifle one of the Mullaneys had been using. He held up the Sharps and said to Denny, "Have you ever fired one of these?"

Denny shuffled his feet. "I, uh, I never fired a gun at all, Mr. Fargo. Cord always said if I tried I'd probably shoot my own foot off."

"The way you're built, I reckon you could handle a Sharps, with a little practice. We'll see about that."

"You mean you're taking us with you?" Cord asked, excitement on his face and in his voice.

"What are you going to do if I don't?"

Cord grinned. "Steal a couple of those horses and follow you anyway."

"That's what I thought. I could have the captain lock you up and take you on to Fort Benton if I wanted to, you know."

"But you're not going to. The odds against you will be bad enough, even with us along. You need our help, Mr. Fargo."

Fargo wasn't so sure about that—but he had been making risky decisions ever since he had gotten involved with the Trahearnes, he reminded himself. Maybe this was no time to stop.

"All right," he said. "You can come with me. But you're in for a hard, dangerous ride, and you'd better be ready to follow my orders without question. If you do that, there's at least a slim chance that we'll all come out of this alive."

Denny smiled. "You mean we're gonna go fight the bad men, Mr. Fargo?"

"That's right, Denny," Fargo said. "We're gonna go fight the bad men."

Taking Cord and Denny with him meant rounding up more supplies, as well as gathering the guns and ammunition that had belonged to the Mullaney brothers. Luckily, they'd had some jerky and hardtack with them, so Fargo just left that in the saddlebags where he found it.

The delay chafed at him, but it really wasn't too long before they were ready to ride. Fargo picked out the biggest of the three horses and gave it to Denny. Cord selected his own mount. When they swung up into their saddles, Fargo had to admit that both of them seemed fairly comfortable on horseback. Most kids growing up on a farm learned how to ride at an early age.

"So long!" he called from the bank to MacGuinness, who stood at the railing on the texas deck. The captain lifted his good hand in a wave of farewell.

Fargo's keen eyes immediately spotted the ruts left by the wheels of three wagons, as well as the hoofprints from a number of horses. He pointed them out to Cord and Denny and said, "That's the trail we'll be following. Keep your eyes on it, but don't forget to watch around you, either. A man who watches the ground all the time can ride right into bad trouble before he knows what's going on."

The reins of the extra horse were tied to Cord's saddlehorn. He studied the tracks and nodded as if he had committed them to memory, then nudged his mount into motion. Denny followed him.

Fargo led the way. The trail angled southwest away from the river. The terrain along the Big Muddy was mostly flat in these parts, arid brown plains with sparse vegetation. Mountains bulked in the distance to both north and south, however, and Fargo knew that the dark blue line along the western horizon represented more mountains. Figuratively speaking, they were on the doorstep of the northern Rockies.

"They're about six hours ahead of us right now," Fargo told Cord and Denny. "We'll cut into their lead today, but we probably won't catch up to them."

"We could ride faster," Cord suggested. "See how these horses run."

"And wear them out so they wouldn't be able to go anywhere tomorrow, and maybe the day after that," Fargo replied with a shake of his head. "The Mullaneys rode those mounts all the way from Saint Louis, I reckon. They're about played out. We'll have to be careful with them."

"What about that stallion of yours?"

"He's stronger," Fargo admitted. "He'd get up and run all day if I let him. But even he can't keep going forever."

"Then we *are* slowing you down," Cord said with a frown.

"Listen," Fargo said. "If I ran the Ovaro flat out all day, yeah, I could catch those outlaws. But out on these flats, they'd see me coming a mile away. The best chance of getting Laurie away from them is if they don't know we're anywhere around until it's too late."

"So we're going to take *days* to catch up to them? For God's sake, Mr. Fargo, anything could happen to her in that time!"

"That's true. But we have to be smart if she's going to have any chance of making it."

Cord clearly didn't like what he was hearing, but he shut up and followed Fargo in silence for a while. Denny made up for it by asking plenty of questions about the plants and animals they saw. The massive youngster was enthralled when a herd of antelope raced by a few hundred yards away, and he was even more impressed when they came across thousands of shaggy buffalo grazing in a broad depression between a couple of shallow bluffs. Fargo reined in atop one of the bluffs and signaled for Cord and Denny to stop. That allowed the horses to rest for a few minutes, and gave Denny a chance to gaze in wonder at the buffalo.

"There must be millions of 'em!" he exclaimed.

"Not in this bunch," Fargo said with a smile as he sat with his hands crossed on the saddlehorn. "This is a very small herd. Some of them do have a million or more buffalo in them. Sometimes when a herd is on the move, you can sit and watch them go by all day, and there's no end to it, stretching as far as the eye can see."

Cord wrinkled his nose. "They smell terrible."

"Be glad you can smell them. If you couldn't, that would mean the wind was the other way and *they* could smell *us*. If they did, they might stampede. This bluff's not tall enough or steep enough to slow them down much if they decided to come this way, and you don't want to be in the path of even a small herd when those critters decide to run a while."

After a few minutes, the three men pushed on. A short time later, Fargo reined in again.

"Why are we stopping now?" Cord asked. "The horses can't need to rest again so soon."

"I was afraid this is what we'd run into," Fargo said. He pointed to the ground ahead of them. "Those buffalo drifted along here after the wagons and the riders came through. The tracks we've been following have been wiped out."

"Does that mean we can't find Laurie?" Denny asked.

"No, but it's going to make our job a little harder. We have to pick up the trail again, on the other side of the path the buffalo followed."

Fargo showed them how the thousands of hooves belonging to the shaggy creatures had obliterated the wagon tracks. The trail had been leading them in a generally southwestward direction, so the best way to start was to continue in that direction, in the hope that their quarry hadn't changed course. Fargo had a good instinct for traveling in a straight line, developed over years of following trails and watching landmarks, so he was able to lead Cord and Denny right to the spot where the trail should have resumed.

Unfortunately, it didn't.

Trying not to show his disgust at their bad luck, Fargo stopped again and explained, "The fact that the trail's not here means that they started in a different direction right where that buffalo herd happened to cross later. We'll have to ride up and down the trail left by the buffalo until we find the wagon tracks again."

"Do you always run into problems like this?" Cord asked.

Fargo had to grin. "So far, this has been an easy trail to follow. They don't believe anybody's going to come after them, so they're not even trying to hide their tracks. That's another reason we don't want them to know we're back here. If they think somebody's following them, they'll try to throw us off the trail."

Fargo started casting along the buffalo path. Within a half hour, he had found the wagon tracks and the hoof-prints of the accompanying riders. The outlaws were headed almost due west now. They had cut far enough south so that their route would take them well south of Fort Benton and on to the mountains.

Again Fargo wondered what was in those crates. Fort Benton was the last settlement for hundreds of miles. What could the raiders be planning to do with that stolen cargo?

One question would answer the other, Fargo thought. Time would answer them both. For now, the important thing was rescuing Laurie.

They ate lunch in the saddle and pushed on. The heat seemed worse out in these arid badlands. Cord and Denny were worn out, and so were their mounts. An hour before dark, Fargo called a halt. Pushing on any farther today would be foolish.

Not surprisingly, Cord argued. "There's still daylight," he said. "I think we should go on while we can."

"Remember what I said about doing what I told you?" Fargo reminded him.

"But they're still way ahead of us!"

"Not as far as they were." Fargo hunkered next to a pile of droppings from a horse or a mule and poked at it with a stick. "Remember how I said they were six hours ahead of us when we started this morning? Well, these droppings were left here about three hours ago, I'd say. That means we've cut their lead in half."

"But if we stop now, they'll get an hour of that back."

"We've still had a productive day. Two more days and we'll be coming up on them." Fargo's lake blue eyes narrowed as he gazed off into the distance. "By then, we'll be getting into the mountains."

That was where the showdown would take place, his gut told him.

While it was still light, Fargo gathered dried buffalo dung to make a small, almost smokeless fire. He brewed coffee, cooked some of the salt pork, and made biscuits.

"We'll put the fire out before it gets dark," he explained to Cord and Denny. "You can see flames for a long way out here, and we don't want to announce to anybody where we are."

"Like Indians?" Cord asked.

Fargo nodded. "That's right."

"I thought you said there weren't any wild Indians, Mr. Fargo," Denny said with a worried look on his face.

"They don't come into Fort Benton." Fargo swept a hand around to indicate their surroundings. "But this is their land, Denny, and we're trying to take it away from them. At least, that's the way they think of it. Of course, they took it away from somebody else, and whoever had it before them took it from somebody else, and that's been the way of it for more years than anybody can count."

"I don't want to take anything away from anybody. I just want us to have a place of our own. As big as everything is out here, there ought to be room for everybody."

"You'd think so, Denny," Fargo agreed. "You'd think so."

Later, as the setting sun painted a spectacular array of

colors in the western sky, Fargo heaped dirt on the fire to put it out. He said to Cord, "We're going to have to take turns standing watch. You reckon you can stay awake for your turn?"

"Sure."

Fargo wasn't convinced, but he didn't say anything. He knew that the Ovaro would warn him if any danger came too close. The stallion would serve as a second sentry without Cord even knowing about it.

"I can be a guard," Denny said.

"That's all right," Fargo told him. "You get some sleep. Maybe you can stand watch tomorrow night."

Denny frowned. He was probably accustomed to people telling him there were all sorts of things he couldn't do, but that didn't mean he had to like it.

When the stars had come out, Fargo told Cord to take the first watch and to wake him at midnight.

"How do I know when that is?" the young man asked.

Fargo pointed out several stars and explained how they would move through the sky and where they would be when it was around midnight. "The sun and the moon and the stars were the first clocks folks ever had," he said, "as well as the first maps. Get to know them, and you'll always have at least some idea of where you are and what time it is."

He and Denny turned in, rolling up in blankets they had brought with them from the *Rockport*. The heat of the day faded almost as soon as the sun went down, and a chill settled over the rugged landscape.

The night passed quietly, except for the howling of some wolves far in the distance. Cord woke Fargo when he was supposed to, then crawled wearily into his own blankets. Fargo roused the brothers early, while the sky was still dark. They tended to the horses and got ready to ride, then Fargo kindled another small fire and prepared a quick, simple breakfast. They were in the saddle and moving as soon as it was light enough to see the trail they were following.

The mountains drew closer during that long day. By noon, Denny said, "We're almost there, aren't we?"

Fargo shook his head. "Those mountains are still a long way off, Denny."

"But they look like they're just right up ahead!"

"Appearances are deceiving, especially out here," Fargo said. He thought about Alexis Rimbard. "You've got to be careful about believing what you think you see."

Cord said, "From the way you talk, a man ought to be careful about everything he does out here."

Fargo looked over at him and nodded. "Now you're starting to understand."

The terrain became rougher, more broken up by ridges and ravines. Obstacles had sometimes forced the wagons they were following to travel a mile or two north or south before they could resume their westward course. That slowed the outlaws even more. When Fargo called a halt that evening and studied the droppings left behind by the wagon teams, he estimated their quarry was no more than an hour ahead of them.

"Then we can catch up to them even earlier tomorrow than you thought," Cord said excitedly when Fargo reported that news.

Fargo shook his head. "We'll do better than catch up. We're going to get ahead of them. They'll come to us."

"What good will that do?"

"We won't really know until we see the lay of the land and figure out our next move," Fargo said, "but it's always better to have the advantage if you can get it."

Denny practically begged to be allowed to stand guard that night. He was desperate to do his part. Fargo agreed.

"You heard what I told Cord last night about how to tell what time it is by looking at the stars?" he asked.

Denny frowned as he tried to concentrate. "I think so," he said, "but I'm not sure I remember all of it . . ."

Patiently, Fargo explained again. He went through it twice, just to be sure that Denny understood. He wasn't too worried, though. Like most veteran frontiersmen, he possessed the ability to wake himself up whenever he needed to. He wouldn't sleep much past midnight, even if Denny didn't wake him.

As it was, though, the hour was earlier than that when Denny placed a hand on Fargo's shoulder and said in a rough whisper, "Mr. Fargo! Mr. Fargo, somethin's wrong!"

Fargo was awake instantly, another ability that men on the frontier were well advised to develop if they wanted to live very long. The Henry rifle, which lay on the ground beside him as he slept, was in his hands by the time he sat up.

"What is it?" he whispered back.

"That horse of yours is actin' like somethin' scared it. And I heard what sounded like a wolf."

Fargo saw the stallion tossing his head up and down and knew that Denny was right—something had spooked him. He wasn't convinced it was a wolf, though.

"How close was the howl?"

"Real close. It scared me."

"You were right to be scared, and right to wake me." Fargo came to his feet and nudged Cord's shoulder with a booted foot. "Cord, get up—"

Before Fargo could finish what he was saying, a sudden screech ripped through the darkness. Several dark shapes seemed to erupt from the ground itself, and as they did so, Fargo knew that the Indians had crawled practically right into their camp. Blackfeet, more than likely.

They hated white men with a passion unmatched by any tribe except maybe the Comanche or the Apache.

He swung the rifle up and fired. The war cry turned into a yelp of pain as one of the attacking figures stumbled. Fargo levered the Henry and fired again. At his feet, Cord scrambled out of his blankets and came up with the Colt he had taken from one of the dead Mullaney brothers. The revolver spouted flame as Cord fired it wildly into the night.

Cord might not hit anything, but at least he was blazing away in the general direction of the Indians and would give them something to think about. Fargo cranked off another couple of rounds and saw one of the warriors stumble. Then the Indians were on them and the quarters were too close for that sort of fighting. Fargo lifted the rifle and drove the butt into one raider's face.

"Get 'em, Denny!" he called. "Don't hold back!"

Denny had to be scared out of his wits, but he responded to Fargo's order. With a rumbling roar, he charged among the Indians and lashed out right and left with his huge fists. The Indians must have thought they were fighting a grizzly bear as he towered over them. Fargo saw Denny grab a warrior by the throat, lift him off the ground, and break his neck with one hard shake.

Then Fargo had his own hands full with a lithe, buckskin-clad Indian trying to brain him with a tomahawk. Fargo used the Henry's barrel to block the blow, then stooped and snatched the Arkansas Toothpick from its sheath on his leg. He brought up the long, heavy blade and drove it home in the Indian's belly, feeling the hot gush of blood over his hand as he ripped the knife one way and then the other. But even dying, the warrior screeched out his hatred and struck again. The flat of the tomahawk caught Fargo on the shoulder and numbed his whole right arm. The knife slipped from his fingers.

He still had the Henry in his left hand. He shoved the gutted Indian away and lashed out at another bounding shape with the rifle. The barrel cracked sharply on a skull and sent the figure tumbling to the ground. Fargo tossed the Henry up, caught it by the barrel, and brought the stock down hard on the back of the Indian's head. Bone crunched.

"Somebody help!" Cord yelled.

Fargo whirled and saw the young man rolling over and over on the ground, locked in a desperate struggle with one of the raiders. The Indian was trying to plant a knife in Cord's chest, and Cord was holding him off with both hands wrapped around the man's wrist.

Before Fargo could spring to Cord's aid, Denny was there. He reached down and grabbed the Indian, tearing him away from Cord. Seemingly effortlessly, Denny lifted the warrior high above his head and then slammed him down on the ground. Fargo heard bones snap like brittle branches.

Denny wasn't done, though. He picked up the luckless Indian again and shook him like a dog shaking a rat. "You hurt my brother!" Denny bellowed. "You hurt my brother!"

After a moment of that, Denny lifted the man above his head again and flung him like a child throwing away a toy. The Indian crashed and skidded across the ground, and then lay limp and motionless.

Fargo looked around and saw that he and Denny were the only ones still on their feet. He hurried over to Cord, who lay there breathing hoarsely and raggedly, and knelt beside him.

"Are you hurt, Cord?" Fargo asked. "That Indian get you with his knife?"

"N-no, I . . . I don't think so. I . . . I'm all right."

Fargo helped Cord sit up. Denny came over to them

and hunkered in front of his brother. He threw his arms around Cord and hugged him tightly. "Cord! You're alive!"

"Yeah, but . . . I won't be . . . if you don't ease up a little! You're crushin' me . . . Denny!"

"Oh!" Denny let go and leaned back. "I'm sorry, Cord."

Fargo helped Cord to his feet. "Stay here with Denny," he said. "I'm going to check on the Indians."

There were six warriors, Blackfeet just as Fargo had suspected. He could tell that from the paint on their faces and the feathers in their hair. And they were all dead, including one who lay near the Ovaro with his head crushed and misshapen. The warrior must have tried to grab the stallion and paid for his mistake with his life. In the confusion, Fargo hadn't seen the Ovaro rear up on his hind legs and strike down the warrior with steel-shod hooves, but he was confident that was what happened. Once the warrior was down, the stallion had made sure that he would never get up again.

"We beat them," Cord said in amazement. "We were outnumbered two to one, and we killed them all."

Actually, Fargo thought, he and Denny had killed the raiders. He didn't figure Cord had hit anything with those wild shots. He would have a talk about that with the young man, but it would have to wait. They had bigger problems now.

"Don't start congratulating yourself," Fargo snapped. "This is bad luck."

"Bad luck?" Cord repeated. "Are you crazy? We're still alive!"

"Yeah, and everybody for miles around heard those shots, too. If these braves were part of a larger war party, the rest of the bunch will be coming along to see what happened. Not only that, but the varmints who stole that cargo and kidnapped Laurie know now that somebody's back here behind them."

Cord frowned in the moonlight. "You mean—"

"I mean getting your sister back safe and sound just got harder," Fargo said.

9

Fargo moved quickly, telling the Trahearne brothers to get their horses saddled and ready to ride.

"I thought you said we couldn't follow the trail in the dark," Cord protested.

"I'm not worried about following the trail," Fargo said. "I'm worried about getting away from the scene of this fight before the rest of that war party shows up looking for them."

"You said there might not be any more of them. It might have been just a little band out hunting or something."

"That's possible," Fargo said, "but I'm not going to bet our lives on it. Let's go. We need to get moving."

Denny said, "I don't want to stay here anyway." He looked at the corpses and shivered. "There's too many dead people here."

Denny was responsible for most of them being dead, Fargo thought, but he didn't point that out. If Denny hadn't made that connection in his own mind, there was no need for Fargo to do it.

Fargo got them ready to ride as quickly as he could, then led them away from the scene of battle. He headed south, at right angles to the course they had been following, and that drew a complaint from Cord.

"Those outlaws are liable to send a few men along their back trail to see what all the shooting was about,"

Fargo said. He was getting tired of having to explain everything to Cord. "We still have a chance of getting ahead of them, but we're going to have to circle a long way around them and ride hard to do it."

"We can ride as hard as we need to, Mr. Fargo," Denny said, "You just tell us where to go and what to do."

"Yeah, I understand," Cord agreed grudgingly. "We'll follow you."

Damned right they would, Fargo thought, or they would get left behind.

He wasn't sure he could do that to Denny, though. The odds of the two of them surviving out here on their own were pretty slim.

The country to the south was even rougher. Fargo led them along gullies, around ridges and mesas, and finally, long after midnight, stopped on a knoll topped with stunted pines. They had a good view of the area around them from up there.

"We'll stay here until dawn and get a little more sleep," he said. "The horses need rest and so do we. Tomorrow will be another long, hard day."

"You think we'll find Laurie tomorrow, Mr. Fargo?" Denny asked.

"I hope so."

"If we do, then it'll all be worth it."

Fargo couldn't argue with that.

He had them moving at first light the next morning. From this higher country, they could look back to the north and see for miles across the broad valley of the Missouri River. Somewhere up there was Fort Benton. The *Rockport* should have reached the settlement by now. Captain MacGuinness might have succeeded in raising a posse to come after the outlaws who had attacked the riverboat, stolen part of its cargo, and kidnapped Laurie Trahearne. Help might be on the way at this very moment.

But Fargo knew better than to count on that. A man had to be prepared to stomp his own snakes.

"How can we get ahead of them when we don't know where they were going?" Cord asked.

"The Missouri curves back into the mountains northwest of here. They've been going in a fairly straight line, and if they keep on in that direction, they'll reach the mountains about the same place as the river does. I think that's where they were headed."

"In other words, it's just a guess."

"A hunch," Fargo said. "I've played them before."

Like the night he had played that hand of showdown with Alexis, the first night on the boat. That hadn't worked out so well, he thought as he smiled wryly to himself. Maybe this hunch would pay off better.

Most of the time, Fargo kept them on the far side of the ridges. He didn't want them skylined, or for sunlight to reflect off their weapons or harness trappings so that it would be visible out on the plains. A glint like that could be seen for miles. Occasionally he stopped, made sure that Cord and Denny were where they couldn't be seen, and then climbed to the top of a hill and bellied down at its crest, his keen eyes searching the miles and miles of landscape spread out before him. He was looking for two things: any sign of a Blackfoot war party pursuing them, or the party of outlaws and their wagons heading toward the Rockies.

Around midafternoon, his eagle-eyed search was finally rewarded. He still didn't see any Indians, for which he was grateful, but he spotted a faint haze of dust in the air, far in the distance. When he focused on that dust, he could barely make out movement at its base. The dust came from the wagons and the riders accompanying them, Fargo knew. After a few minutes, he could even make out the vehicles themselves, as the heavily loaded vehicles continued their slow trek westward.

By cutting south as he and the Trahearne brothers had, Fargo had made it impossible for the outlaws to tell if they were being pursued or not. If some of them had gone back to check and found the corpses of the Blackfoot warriors, they would see that the hoofprints of the survivors led south. For all the outlaws knew, the fight had nothing to do with them.

Anyway, there was a limit to how fast they could push those wagon teams. Fargo felt a surge of confidence because he knew that he and his companions had regained the advantage. They were ahead of the wagons.

He slid back down the hill to join Cord and Denny. "They're back there," he announced.

"The men who took Laurie?" Denny asked.

"That's right."

"Well, let's go get her."

Fargo shook his head. "It's not that simple. We're going to wait for them to come to us, remember?"

"Oh, yeah," Denny said. "Sorry. I forgot."

"Nothing to be sorry about," Fargo told him. "Let's go."

They kept their horses moving at a fast pace. The animals were reaching the limits of their strength, even the Ovaro. Fargo hoped they wouldn't have to make a hard run to get away from the outlaws once they had freed Laurie from her captivity. That might prove difficult.

By the time the sun began to lower toward the mountains behind them, Fargo, Cord, and Denny were on a boulder-littered ridge high above the mouth of the canyon where the Missouri River entered the Rockies. To the right bulked a range of smaller peaks known as the Big

Belt Mountains; behind them the river flowed through a gap called MacDonald Pass. Fargo knew this rugged country well. In front of them, the ridge dropped off in a sheer cliff about a hundred feet high. At the base of the cliff was a fairly steep, wooded slope that flowed on down to a large, grassy park. In the Shining Times, mountain men had sometimes held their rendezvous at that park. Before that, Indian tribes had gotten together there to parley. It was a good place to meet.

Fargo wondered if Emory, Alexis, and the rest of the outlaws were going to meet someone there.

"What are we going to do now?" Cord asked as the three of them lay on a sloping slab of rock, looking toward the approaching wagons.

"That depends on what they do," Fargo replied. "We'll wait right here until we have a better idea of what their plans are." He paused. "They won't be going any deeper into the mountains tonight, though. They'll stop down below in that park."

"Then tonight would be a good time to get Laurie away from them, wouldn't it?" Cord looked around. "If we could get her back up here and hide in the mountains, they'd have a hard time finding us."

"There's more to it than that," Fargo said. "Rescuing Laurie is the most important thing, but I want to find out what's so important about those crates they took off the *Rockport*."

Cord shook his head. "No matter what they're up to, you can't fight the whole gang, Mr. Fargo. Let's get Laurie, and then maybe you can bring the army back here and have them handle it. The stuff belonged to the army to begin with, didn't it?"

"Hard to say when we don't know what's in the crates. Anyway, by the time the army could get here, it would be too late. Emory and the others would be long gone."

If Emory was still alive, he added to himself. That was another thing he was mighty curious about.

The outriders reached the park a short time later, followed by the wagons and the rest of the horsemen. Fargo watched intently and picked out the shining blond hair of Alexis Rimbard. She rode next to the driver on the first wagon. Laurie was on the seat of the second wagon. Denny started to stand up when he saw her, but Fargo caught his sleeve and tugged him back down.

"What were you going to do?" Fargo asked.

"I was gonna wave and holler down there to Laurie so she'd see me." Denny frowned in thought. "That would've been the wrong thing to do, wouldn't it?"

"I know you're glad to see her, but for now we have to be quiet and not let any of them know that we're up here, not even Laurie."

Denny nodded. "I understand."

Fargo understood, too. Denny was just glad to see Laurie. So was he. As best he could tell from this distance, the outlaws hadn't harmed her, but of course, it was difficult to be sure about that.

The tall, broad-shouldered owlhoot Captain MacGuinness had mentioned was with the outriders. He had been the first one into the park. Now he wheeled his horse and rode back to the wagons. He wore a black, wide-brimmed hat and a long coat made out of what appeared to be buffalo hide. He reined in next to the second wagon, dismounted, and lifted Laurie down from the seat, handling her as if she were a doll rather than a human being. He pointed and spoke to her, but Fargo had no idea what he was saying.

Meanwhile, Alexis had climbed down from the driver's seat of the first wagon. She went to the back of the vehicle, where a figure was stretched out on a crude pallet among the crates of stolen cargo. That was Emory, Fargo thought. The past three days must have been a hellishly hard ride for the man who was carrying one of Fargo's bullets in his body.

Several outlaws came up and took Emory out of the wagon, carrying him to some blankets spread out under a tree. They put him down carefully on the blankets. Even at this distance, Fargo could make out the bloodstained bandages tied around the treacherous officer's midsection. Fargo's shot had caught Emory in the belly, the sort of wound that caused a long, lingering, agonizing death. It was a miracle that Emory was still alive. By now the renegade major probably wished he had died instantly when he was shot.

The men began unhitching the mule teams and making camp. "From the looks of it, they're settling in to wait for somebody," Fargo said to Cord and Denny.

"Another of those hunches of yours?" Cord asked.

"Why come all this way otherwise?"

Cord didn't have an answer for that.

Fargo watched as Alexis walked over and spoke briefly to Emory. He kept an eye on Laurie, as well. She sat down under a tree. The big boss outlaw stood next to her, talking to her. Laurie nodded from time to time. She wasn't tied up—but if she ran away, where could she go? They were in the middle of a vast, untamed wilderness filled with wild animals and wilder Indians.

Shadows began stealing over the park. Cord said, "Are we going to wait until it's good and dark, then go down there and get her?"

"I am," Fargo said. "You and Denny are going to stay up here."

"We can help—"

"You can help the most by doing what I tell you," Fargo said bluntly. "Besides, if there's trouble, I'll be counting on the two of you to help Laurie and me get out of there."

"Well . . . that makes sense, I guess."

Denny asked, "How are you gonna get down there, Mr. Fargo? I don't think you can climb down that cliff."

"That's where you come in," Fargo told him with a smile. "I brought some rope with us from the riverboat. You're going to lower me down, Denny, and when I get back with Laurie, you'll have to haul her up."

Denny nodded. "I can do that."

"Cord, you'll have the Henry. If we need covering fire, you'll have to give it to us."

"Sure. We've got a good angle from up here."

"That's why I picked the place," Fargo said. "I've slipped into enemy camps before, but they're going to be on guard, so it'll be risky. We'll need some luck on our side."

"I'll give you all the luck I got, Mr. Fargo," Denny said.

Fargo chuckled. "I appreciate that, but you'd better save a little bit of it for yourself, Denny. You're liable to need it."

They waited as the shadows grew thicker and gloom settled over the landscape. Down below in the park, the outlaws built a large campfire. That was unusual in these parts. Most folks wouldn't want to announce their presence like that while there were hostiles around. That made a new suspicion stir in the back of Fargo's mind.

Darkness fell fairly quickly. Fargo worried that the light from the campfire would reach the cliff, but when he led Cord and Denny to the edge and looked over, he saw that the glow fell short. The cliff was dark enough so that it was unlikely anybody would spot him as he descended.

He played out the coil of rope he had brought with him and ran it around the trunk of a pine before tying it around Denny's waist. "The tree will take most of the weight," he explained. "All you have to do right now is hold it steady.

I'll climb down myself. When I bring Laurie back, though, you'll have to lift her up."

"I can do it," Denny said. "You don't have to worry, Mr. Fargo."

"I'm not worried," Fargo said as he smiled and clapped a hand on Denny's shoulder.

Cord held the fully loaded Henry. "How will I know if I need to start shooting?" he asked.

"Don't open fire unless I tell you to," Fargo said. "Or if they start shooting first. If we can get Laurie out of there without any gunplay, though, all the better."

Cord nodded. "All right." He paused. "Good luck, Mr. Fargo."

"Good luck to you boys, too," Fargo said. He threw the other end of the rope over the edge of the cliff.

After making sure that the rope wouldn't be rubbing against a rough spot on the rocks that might cause it to fray, Fargo took hold of it in both hands, sat down on the brink, and turned so that he could slide off. For a second he was dangling in space, a hundred feet up, suspended only by the grip of his hands. Then he got the soles of his boots against the cliff's rocky face and found some tiny footholds.

Climbing down the sheer cliff in the dark like that was pretty harrowing. The darkness was helpful in a way, though, because Fargo couldn't see how far off the ground he was. He let himself down hand over hand, supporting as much of his weight with his feet as he could.

Time didn't have much meaning in a situation like that. He couldn't afford to rush, but he didn't linger, either. Eventually, even in the darkness, he saw trees around him and knew he was almost at the bottom. A few moments later, he felt the sloping ground under his feet.

He gave the rope a tug to let Denny know that he was down, then let go of it. He had to be careful heading down the slope, which was still pretty steep even though it wasn't sheer like the cliff. There were plenty of bushes and trees to hold on to, though, when he needed something to help him keep his balance.

When Fargo reached the edge of the trees, he stopped and hunkered next to the trunk of a pine where he was still in deep shadow. He watched the outlaws, who were sitting around the fire eating and drinking. The big man had a graying spade beard and a gaunt face with deep-set eyes. Fargo didn't recognize him.

Laurie sat alone on a wagon tongue, picking at a plate of beans. Fargo didn't see Alexis and wondered if she was back in one of the other wagons with Emory.

The outlaws didn't seem to be posting any guards. That was probably because none of them appeared to be getting ready to turn in for the night. They were all still awake and alert. A festive atmosphere lay over the camp, like this was a celebration of sorts.

The grass in the park was lush and tall enough so that Fargo could crawl through it unseen. He took his hat off, left it under the tree, and started forward on his belly, using his elbows and toes to inch himself toward the wagons. No one was paying much attention to Laurie. If he could get close enough to call out softly to her, she might be able to slip off without anyone noticing. Even if someone in the camp raised the alarm, Fargo thought they would stand a good chance of getting away if they reached the base of the cliff in time for Denny to haul Laurie up. Of course, it would be more difficult for him to climb back up that rope if somebody was shooting at him. . . .

Maybe that wouldn't happen, he told himself. If they could get away into the mountains before the outlaws knew Laurie was gone, Fargo was confident he could keep them ahead of any pursuit.

But that wouldn't solve the mystery of what was in those crates, he thought, or why the cargo had been stolen in the first place. If things came down to it, he might have to trade those answers for Laurie's life. He was willing to do that, even though he didn't like the idea.

Keeping his head down except for the occasional check to make sure no one had spotted him, Fargo crawled closer and closer to the outlaw camp. He was within fifty yards of Laurie now, as she sat with her back toward him.

Suddenly he felt a faint vibration in the ground and recognized it for what it was. Riders were coming—a large number of riders. Fargo froze, hugging the ground and waiting to see what was going to happen.

Shouts of greeting sounded from the camp. Fargo lifted his head enough to see at least fifty Indians ride in, their faces painted for war. More Blackfeet, he thought, perhaps even the band those other warriors had come from. Instead of attacking the white men who were camped here, though, they raised their hands in the symbol for peace and dismounted. A warrior whose elaborate headdress identified him as the chief strode over to the boss outlaw and embraced him. The two men pounded each other on the back.

That didn't particularly surprise Fargo. The reason the outlaws hadn't been afraid to build a big fire was because they weren't afraid of the Indians. That meant they were expecting this Blackfoot war party.

And that couldn't be a good thing.

The boss outlaw brought the chief over to the wagon where Laurie sat. She shrank back from the fierce-looking warrior, causing both the Indian and the outlaw to laugh. The outlaw reached into the back of the wagon and took hold of one of the crates. His powerful muscles hauled it out with ease and dropped it on the ground. The lid broke from the impact. The outlaw kicked the lid aside, reached into the crate, and brought out a rifle. A Henry repeater, from the looks of it. He held it out to the chief, who laughed and took the weapon.

Fargo's jaw tightened. So at least some of the crates held rifles, just as both he and Captain MacGuinness had suspected. And from the looks of things, those rifles were about to be sold to the Indians.

The problem with that was that the Indians didn't have money to pay for the weapons. So it had to be a barter of some sort, but what did the Blackfeet possess that would be worth it for the white men to trade the rifles?

The Blackfoot chief ran his hands over the rifle with the sort of look on his face a man usually wore when he was caressing a woman. He looked at the boss outlaw and nodded. Then he gestured toward Laurie and said something. Fargo could hear the coarse, guttural voice but couldn't make out the words.

He heard the outlaw, though, when the man said, "The girl wasn't part of the deal, Chief."

The Indian spoke again and stabbed a finger toward Laurie, who stood up and started to back away nervously. Suddenly, the chief lunged forward and grabbed her arm, jerked her toward him. The boss outlaw swept his buffalo coat back and started to reach for the gun on his hip. Around the camp, the rest of the gang tensed. Rifles came up. The other Indians reacted to the sudden tension, as well. They lifted lances, bows, and old, single-shot rifles. They outnumbered the white men by more than two to one. Even though the outlaws were better armed, if a fight started, the Blackfeet would probably wipe them out.

The boss outlaw had to know that. He stopped his draw before his gun ever left its holster. Stiffly, he stepped away from Laurie and gave the chief a curt nod.

"Take her," he said, giving in to the chief's demand.

Fargo felt a pang of disappointment. He had thought

for a second that if a ruckus broke out, he would dash in while the outlaws and the Indians were all trying to kill each other, grab Laurie, and get her out of there in the confusion. Clearly, though, that wasn't going to happen. The boss outlaw was prepared to give her up to get whatever it was he wanted.

That had to come as even more of a shock to Laurie, because as the chief started to drag her away, she looked back at the boss outlaw and screamed, "Pa! Don't let him take me! *Pa!*"

Fargo felt almost like he'd been punched in the gut. The leader of the outlaws was *Isaac Trahearne*? Laurie, Cord, and Denny's father?

In a way it made sense. Trahearne had come west to make his fortune, and according to Cord, he had always been one to take the easy way out. It wasn't all that surprising he had become an outlaw. Coincidence had put his children on the same riverboat he intended to rob, and while some people claimed not to believe in coincidence, Fargo had seen it happen too many times not to believe in it.

Laurie was still screaming as the Blackfoot chief tried to drag her away. Trahearne stood by stiffly, doing nothing, letting the chief take his daughter.

Suddenly, Laurie twisted in the Indian's grip and clawed at his face with both hands. He grunted in pain and let go of her. She turned and ran, hurdling the wagon tongue where she had been sitting earlier and sprinting away from the camp.

Straight toward Fargo.

Well, when things are already going to hell, Fargo thought, the only thing to do is to bust them open even wider. He rose from the grass, palming the Colt as he did so, and shouted, "Laurie! This way!"

It must have been surprise at seeing him that caused her to break stride momentarily, but the stumble lasted only a second. Then she came on, running as hard as she could. The Blackfoot chief had come after her, still carrying the rifle from the crate. When he saw Fargo, he stopped, threw the rifle to his shoulder, and pulled the trigger.

Nothing happened. The Henry wasn't loaded, of course. But the chief hadn't thought of that.

He didn't have time to think of anything else, because a split second after that, a bullet from the Trailsman's .44 crashed through his brain and knocked him backward.

The other members of the war party didn't know what was going on, but they had just seen their chief gunned down by a white man, so they reacted the only way they knew how. They opened fire on the nearest white men, in this case, the outlaws who had stolen the cargo from the *Rockport* and brought it to this remote mountain park.

The outlaws dashed for cover, firing pistols and rifles as they ran. Most of them made it, but several tumbled to the ground, their bodies bristling with arrows. The Indians charged their ponies among the outlaws, riding down some of them, skewering others with lances. Many of the warriors fell as well, blasted off their mounts by the outlaws' gunfire.

Fargo heard the Henry cracking from the top of the cliff as Cord opened fire on the camp. With Laurie out of the line of fire and any need for stealth gone, Fargo was glad that Cord had started shooting. In all the chaos, it was possible that none of the men battling in the camp would even notice where those rounds were coming from. Fargo didn't know if Cord was aiming at outlaws, Indians, or both. It didn't really matter. Under the circumstances, any of them he could kill would be just fine.

Fargo turned and ran after Laurie. His longer legs allowed him to catch up to her as she reached the trees. She must have heard him coming, because she looked back over her shoulder, her face contorted with fear as if the Devil himself were after her.

"Skye! What—"

Fargo grabbed her arm and hurried her along. "Time for explanations later," he told her. "We've got to get up that cliff!"

Panting with exertion, they climbed the slope until they reached the bottom of the cliff. Even in the darkness, Fargo had brought them back to the spot where the rope still dangled. He holstered his gun, took hold of the rope, and wrapped it around Laurie's body, tying it under her arms.

Then he tugged hard on the rope, stepped back, cupped his hands around his mouth, and shouted, "Haul her up, Denny!"

Laurie started to say, "Denny's up—" Then she said, "Oh!" as her feet left the ground.

"Use your arms and legs to keep from banging into the cliff," Fargo called up to her.

She got the hang of fending herself away from the cliff fairly quickly as she rose through the air. Fargo drew the Colt again and turned back toward the camp, in case anyone had followed them. The outlaws and the Indians were too busy trying to kill each other to worry about anything else, though.

"Mr. Fargo!" Cord shouted. "Here comes the rope!"

Fargo looked up, saw the rope end tumbling toward him. He snagged it as it fell beside him and holstered the Colt again. Using both hands, he started climbing.

He was about halfway up, with another fifty feet to go, when a bullet spanged off the rocky cliff beside him. A second later, another slug smacked into the cliff and showered him with rock splinters. Fargo twisted his head and saw Isaac Trahearne's towering figure standing atop the cargo in one of the wagons. At least two arrows protruded from the man's body, which was lit up by the fire burning behind him. Trahearne had to be dying, but he was doing his damnedest to take Fargo across the divide with him. As Fargo watched, Trahearne levered another round in the firing chamber of the rifle he held and squeezed off a shot. The bullet whined off the cliff no more than two feet from Fargo.

"Keep climbing, Mr. Fargo!" Cord yelled from above. "I've got the Sharps! I'll get him!"

Cord hadn't ever fired the Sharps, so Fargo didn't hold out much hope of him being able to hit Trahearne. But miracles sometimes happened, so Fargo kept climbing. Another bullet whistled past his ear.

Above him, the Sharps boomed. As Fargo twisted his head again to look, the thought crossed his mind that Cord might not be aware he had just shot at his own father. If Laurie hadn't said anything, then Cord had no way of knowing. . . .

Trahearne flew backward as if a giant hand had just slapped him down. He landed among the crates and didn't move. Against all odds, Cord had made the shot.

And probably killed his father at the same time.

Fargo continued hauling himself up as fast as he could. A few moments later, he reached the top and sprawled over the edge. Laurie was there to help him to his feet. As she did, she said in a low, urgent voice, "Cord doesn't know. Neither of them do."

Fargo nodded. The identity of the boss outlaw was Laurie's secret, to tell or not.

She wasn't through, though. She said, "Those kegs in the third wagon are full of blasting powder. That's part of what this was all about."

Fargo wanted to hear about that, but for the time being they had other problems to deal with. He looked at the camp and saw that the Indians were finishing off the last of the outlaws. One more shot rang out, and then the warriors began swarming over the wagons, tearing into the crates to see what booty they had just captured.

"Cord," Fargo said, "give me that Sharps."

Cord handed over the heavy rifle. Fargo had some of the long, deadly cartridges in his pocket. Moving with swift, practiced assurance, he pulled out one of the cartridges and reloaded the rifle.

He had been confident that he could give the outlaws the slip in the mountains, even with Laurie, Cord, and Denny accompanying him. The Blackfeet were a different story. If the Indians were on their trail, the deck would be stacked against Fargo and his companions, even though it appeared more than half the war party had been killed in the battle.

But at the moment the remaining Indians had all gathered around the wagons, which were parked close together. Quite a few of them, in fact, were *in* that third wagon.

Fargo brought the Sharps to his shoulder, took a deep breath, held it, lined the sights, and squeezed the trigger. With a dull boom, the Sharps kicked against his shoulder.

With a much larger boom, the kegs of blasting powder exploded.

There were boxes full of ammunition for the rifles down there, too, and the explosion set them off as well. A huge ball of flame blossomed in the night. Screaming, burning men flew through the air. The wagon that had held the blasting powder was gone, blown to smithereens. As debris thrown high in the air began to pelt back down, Fargo saw that only a handful of the Indians were still moving around, and some of them were probably badly injured. He and his companions didn't have to worry about the war party anymore.

As Fargo lowered the Sharps, which still had tendrils of smoke curling from its muzzle, Laurie put her arms around him and said, "Skye, I don't know where you came from, but I was never so glad to see anyone in my life!" She turned to hug her brothers. "And you, and you! Cord, Denny . . . I can't believe it. I . . . I thought I was doomed."

"Mr. Fargo did it," Cord said. "He's the one who found you. He wouldn't let those bastards get away with kidnapping you."

Laurie glanced at Fargo, who returned the look impassively. It was still up to her what she said—or didn't say. Up here on the cliff, Cord and Denny wouldn't have been able to hear her when she screamed at her father for giving her to the Blackfoot chief.

She turned back to her brothers and smiled. "Let's go home," she said.

"But we don't have a home," Denny said with a frown.

"Yes, we do, honey," she told him. "Yes, we do." She turned and looked out over the fire that was still burning brightly below. "We just haven't found it yet."

"It was all about the gold," Laurie said the next day as the four of them rode toward Fort Benton. Fargo hadn't pressured her for any explanations the night before, but he still wanted answers and he figured she might have gotten them during the time she had spent with the outlaws.

"What gold?" Fargo asked.

"The gold that an army scouting party found in the mountains not far from here," Laurie said.

Fargo shook his head. "I hadn't heard about that."

"Neither have most people. According to Major Emory, the army is trying to keep it quiet because they don't want a gold rush up here. They're already stretched too thin on the frontier as it is, and they think if a lot of prospectors pour in, the situation with the Indians will just get worse."

"They're probably right about that," Fargo said. "I reckon Emory found out about it, anyway."

"That's right. He and that sergeant of his set up the whole thing. They managed to steal a shipment of guns and ammunition. The soldiers who were with them on the *Rockport* helped them."

"Huh," Fargo said. "I figured they weren't in on the plan."

"They were in on it, all right," Laurie said, "Emory just double-crossed them. He arranged with those outlaws that the troops would be killed as soon as they came on board the riverboat."

"Emory got tied in with the outlaws through Alexis Rimbard?"

Laurie nodded. "Yes. She knew . . . the man in charge of the gang. She'd met him in Fort Benton and knew he was just the sort of man who'd be willing to work with Emory. I don't know how she got involved with Emory."

"No telling," Fargo said with a shake of his head. "I don't reckon we'll ever know that."

"I'm gettin' confused," Denny said. "The soldiers were bad? I didn't even know there *were* any soldiers."

"These soldiers turned bad," Fargo explained. "They were greedy and forgot about their duty."

"Oh. I understand . . . I guess."

Fargo knew how the youngster felt. He had never quite understood how greed could make a man abandon his honor, either.

He turned back to Laurie and went on, "I guess they had supplies and mining equipment in those crates, too, like that blasting powder, as well as the guns they were going to trade to the Indians."

"That's right," she said.

"Wait a minute," Cord said. "Trade for what?"

"Their own safety," Fargo guessed. He looked to Laurie for confirmation, and she nodded. "The outlaws made a deal with the Blackfoot chief. They would turn those rifles over to him, and he and the rest of the tribe wouldn't bother them while they were digging for gold. They'd get a jump on everybody else and make a fortune before anyone even knew there was gold in the mountains."

"But the Indians would have taken those guns and wiped out a bunch of other people!" Cord said. "They might have even attacked Fort Benton."

Fargo nodded. "Yep. But Emory and the rest of the bunch didn't care. All they cared about was getting their hands on as much gold as they could."

"That's crazy," Denny said.

"No. Just evil."

"Well, it won't happen now," Laurie said. "Thanks to the three of you."

Cord had an excited look on his face. "Maybe *we* should go look for gold," he suggested. "We could get rich."

"You could lose your hair, too," Fargo pointed out. "There are plenty of other Indians in these parts who aren't going to like it when folks come in and start digging up their mountains."

"Yeah, but it's only a matter of time until that happens anyway," Cord argued. "We can be first."

"I think you'd be better off starting a store in Fort Benton, or something like that. When news of the gold leaks out—and you're right, it's just a matter of time—there'll be a lot of men going through there, and they'll all need supplies. That's the way it always is in a gold rush. A handful of prospectors make a fortune, and everybody else breaks their back for little or nothing. But the folks who supply them, they wind up doing all right."

"Well . . ." Cord still didn't sound convinced.

"I think I'd like to have a store," Denny said.

Laurie laughed. "You know, I think I would, too."

"You people just don't know how to gamble!"

Denny said solemnly, "I think my gamblin' days are over. And I'm mighty tired of fightin', too."

Laurie reached over and squeezed his arm. "We'll try to see to it that you never have to fight again, Denny."

Cord heaved a sigh. "All right. We'll be storekeepers, instead."

Fargo hoped the young man would follow through on that.

He had his doubts, though.

Captain F. X. MacGuinness wasn't wearing his arm in a sling anymore as he sat at a table in a Fort Benton saloon and shared a bottle of whiskey with Fargo a couple of days later. He shook his head and said, "Good Lord, what a story."

"Which you promised you'd keep to yourself," Fargo reminded him.

MacGuinness nodded. "Oh, I will, I will. I'm a man of my word. But you know what's going to happen sooner or later, Fargo. We both do."

Fargo looked down into his glass and nodded. "Yeah." He had seen gold rushes before. To a man like him, who had fallen in love with the wild, untamed West years before, who enjoyed its vast solitudes and its harsh, unforgiving beauty, there was nothing worse than a gold rush, with men swarming over the land like ants, chipping away at it, raising a racket, fouling the streams, bringing all their vice and ugliness with them so that things were never the same.

But, of course, there was nothing he could do to stop it. All he could do was cling to what was slowly vanishing as long as he could.

"What are Miss Trahearne and her brothers going to do?" MacGuinness asked.

"They plan to settle here in Fort Benton."

"Good. They're solid folks. Well, Miss Laurie and Denny are. Fort Benton can use them."

"Cord will come around," Fargo said. "Laurie will see to that."

"I hope you're right." MacGuinness downed the last of his drink. "Well, I'd best be getting back to the docks. The *Rockport* will be leaving first thing in the morning." He grinned. "Want a ride back to Saint Louis? We can find the room."

Fargo laughed and shook his head. "No thanks. I've had enough of towns for a while. And, no offense, enough of riverboats, too."

"Some of us never get enough of riverboats," MacGuinness said as he stood up. "So long, Fargo."

"So long, Captain."

There was only a little whiskey left in the bottle. Fargo poured it in his glass, savored the last few sips. Outside, night had fallen. He thought for a moment about sitting in on the poker game that was going on in the corner of the saloon, then decided against it. He decided he would go back to the hotel where he had taken a room and turn in for the night—even though in a way he dreaded it.

He was afraid that a blond phantom would haunt his dreams again.

He hadn't seen what happened to Alexis during the fight at the outlaws' camp, but he couldn't imagine that she had survived. The Blackfeet had wiped out all the whites before they started pawing through the cargo in the wagons. And that bothered him. Sure, she had betrayed him and helped set in motion a chain of events that included a great deal of death and destruction. Still, he hated the fact that she must have died in pain and terror.

Fargo shouldered through the batwings and turned to the left, toward the hotel. There were no boardwalks in Fort Benton; the buildings opened out into the street, which was a sea of mud in the winter and ankle deep in dust in the summer, like now. He saw the *Rockport* tied up at the dock, about a hundred and fifty yards away. A rider plodded between him and the boat.

"Skye . . ."

Fargo stopped short. Had he imagined it? A woman's voice calling his name in the faintest whisper. He looked toward the shadows between a couple of buildings, thought he saw a flicker of movement there.

The voice might have been his imagination.

The metallic ratcheting of a gun being cocked behind him sure as hell wasn't.

Fargo lunged sideways, whipping around as the gun roared. He heard the bullet sing past his ear. The Colt was in his hand by now, without him even having to think about it, and as he saw the figure on horseback fire again, muzzle flame spurting in the night, the .44 roared and bucked in his hand. The rider jerked back as Fargo's bullet struck him, but he didn't fall. Instead he fired again, the slug plowing up dust at Fargo's feet. Fargo triggered a second time. The rider threw out his arms and went backward off the skittish horse, landing on his back in the road. Dust puffed up in a cloud around him.

Fargo hurried over, kicked the fallen gun away. The light that spilled through the saloon's windows showed him a bald head and a familiar face. The sergeant who had worked for Major Emory. —

Fargo had never even known the man's name, and now he'd killed him.

But if the sergeant had made it through the battle with the Indians somehow, then that meant—

Fargo whirled toward the shadows where he thought

he had seen movement and heard the woman's voice. He ran over to the gap between the buildings, thinking even as he did so that he was being reckless, taking a foolish chance. But nothing happened, and when Fargo fished a lucifer from his pocket and snapped it to life with his thumbnail, the harsh glare from the match revealed . . . nothing. The alley was empty.

Men came from the saloon and shouted questions in the night. Fargo didn't have any answers for them, or for himself.

But as he stood there with the smoking .44 in his hand, he thought back to what Laurie Trahearne had told her brothers when they got to Fort Benton and asked when they were going to start looking for their father.

"Cord, Denny . . . I didn't want to tell you this, but . . . the leader of that outlaw gang . . . he knew Pa . . . he told me that Pa died more than a year ago."

Some things, maybe it was better just not knowing.

LOOKING FORWARD!
The following is the opening
section of the next novel in the exciting
***Trailsman* series from Signet:**

THE TRAILSMAN #336
UTAH OUTLAWS

Tall Rock, Utah Territory, 1860—
a town where greed and murder go hand in hand
and lead straight to the graveyard on the edge of town.

Skye Fargo started noticing his dizziness when the stage-coach was about eight miles out of Tall Rock.

His first thought was that the gristly steak he'd eaten right before taking up his position on the run was making him queasy.

Fargo was the only passenger on this trip. He was a very special passenger. Three weeks ago this same stage had been held up by robbers. A large amount of money had been taken, bank money intended for another bank eighty miles away.

Fargo had been hired by his old friend Henry Granger, the man who owned the stage line, to make sure that didn't happen again. On this trip, Fargo hid in the coach, armed with his Henry and Colt. His lake blue eyes scanned the countryside first from one door and then the other.

But as the coach moved forward in the shadows of the Wellsville Mountain Range here in northern Utah, he started getting even sicker. He knew how important this run was to Henry. Lee Whitney, one of the bank's owners, had wanted to use his own buckboard with his own guards to transport this shipment of money to the other bank but Henry had convinced him that with Fargo hiding on board there wouldn't be any problems. Fargo could handle any trouble that came along.

The trouble was . . . how much help would Fargo be if he was vomiting his guts out?

A man named Newly Davis drove the stage. Since fall was his favorite season he should have been enjoying himself. But as Hap Miller, the older man riding shotgun noted, Newly looked more agitated than usual. Miller spent a lot of time smiling when he rode with Newly. The thirty-five-year-old worried about everything. So far he'd managed to stew over the axle, the traces, the right rear wheel. Nothing was wrong with any of them, of course. But Newly never seemed happy unless he was making himself—and everybody around him—miserable.

Miller was glad Fargo was on board. Miller had been the shotgun man when the stage had been held up the last time. He'd almost gotten himself killed. The robbers had shot one of the horses, grinding the stage to a halt. The smaller robber had jumped on the back of the vehicle and worked his way up top, surprising Miller. The other man had been firing at Miller to distract him and the plot had worked well. The short man with the blond hair had leaped on Miller and begun pistol-whipping him with such ferocity that his partner shouted, "No killing! Leave him be!"

Whoever the blond man had been—and behind that red bandana of a mask, Miller suspected was a very young man—he'd been clearly insane. The sounds he'd made while pistol-whipping Miller had been almost sexual in their pleasure.

But Miller rested easy. He knew of the Trailsman's reputation and he had Henry's personal word that Fargo would surprise the hell out of anybody who tried to rob them this time.

So Hap was feeling pretty damned good until he glanced behind the stage and saw the two riders coming down fast from a small timbered hill behind them. They were coming damned fast and if he wasn't mistaken their faces were covered with bandanas . . .

Robert Wilks knew that Billy Clute was mad at him and he didn't give a damn.

As they galloped toward the stagecoach, he could still hear Billy, even above the pounding hooves of their horses, cursing to himself about what he called Wilks' "preaching."

But in order to make Billy understand anything you had to repeat it over and over again. Billy wasn't stupid. He just had the ability to block out anything he didn't want to hear. So when the orders came to rob this stage and make sure that nobody was hurt, Wilks set about repeating the second part of the orders several times a day. And Billy resented it.

But to hell with Billy. Last time the kid had damned

near beaten the shotgun man to death with his Colt. And he would have, too, if Wilks hadn't dragged him out of his frenzy. Once Billy got into one of his violent moments, he was terrifying to watch.

Wilks enjoyed the fear and anxiety of holdups whether they were inside banks or out on rocky stage roads. He felt alive and young despite his otherwise weary forty-three years. His one long stretch in prison his dreams came in two forms—of long-legged, full-breasted women and of robberies, him with the gun and a line of citizens with their hands up and their eyes wide and their bodies trembling.

He wasn't some dirt-poor lowlife at these moments; he was somebody important enough to buffalo all these people.

The only thing he had to worry about now was keeping Billy from doing something stupid . . .

When Fargo heard the horses pounding toward them, he forced himself up from the seat where he'd collapsed a few minutes ago. The chills and the nausea had overwhelmed him. He'd actually heard his teeth chattering.

He clutched his Henry. He would open fire with that and then switch to his Colt if they managed to get in range. He had been through so many situations like this that he shouldn't have any trouble at all with them.

But he had to be able to focus his eyes better . . . and he had to swallow down the bitter bile that was threatening to explode from him . . . and he had to have the strength to pick up the Henry and point it and . . .

He fell back on the seat again. He was so dizzy he wondered if he would even be able to sit up, let alone stand up.

The strange taste of the steak was sharp in his throat and mouth. Had somebody drugged the meat?

Then—the horses. Then—gunshots.

Had to sit up . . . had to get the Henry and . . .

As they drew near the stagecoach, Wilks cut wide.

About the only thing Wilks had ever done that impressed the smirking Clute was showing him how to rob a stage. When there was only one man riding shotgun, one robber got ahead of the stage and the other came up from behind. It didn't take long for the shotgun man to decide that fighting two shooters from opposite directions was foolishness. And certain to cost him his life.

The only part of it that Clute didn't like was that nine out of ten times the shotgun man laid his guns down and raised his arms in surrender. Clute would have preferred to kill him. He didn't like to have his fun spoiled.

But as Wilks raced ahead of the stage and then reined his horse in for the fast ride back, he could see that the shotgun man was busy ducking the bullets that Clute was pumping over the man's head with his repeater. And that was the strict order both their employer and Wilks had given him. Stay out of range and you won't have any need to kill him. Just keep him busy until I start back toward the stage. And start firing myself.

The shotgun man's curses were almost as loud as his bullets as the stage jerked and jostled along the rough and narrow road.

Wilks got his horse turned around just in time to see it happen.

The shot didn't sound like anything special. Just one of several that Clute fired a few feet above the shotgun man's head.

But this one—this one—ripped the top of the man's head off. A bloody hairy mass rising inches off his skull and a single interminable scream cleaving the air. And in that moment—frozen and immortal in the life of Robert Kevin Wilks—he became what he'd never been before . . . an accessory to murder. A grifter, a thief, a burglar, a bank robber, a counterfeiter . . . these were all crimes that Wilks claimed without anything approaching a guilty conscience.

But he'd never come close to murdering anybody or even being around the violent death of another human being. Until now.

The driver drew the stage to a halt. Ghosts of dust from the road rose up. The four horses whinnied.

Now that the stage was stopped, the driver just about threw himself onto the dead man, shouting, "Hap! Hap! Hap! Talk to me, Hap!" He sounded insane.

Wilks drew up close to the stage and dropped from his horse. Clute came around the vehicle on his mount. His lips didn't smirk but his eyes did. "Guess I winged him."

In the eight months since they'd met they'd made several successful scores, three banks and the first stagecoach a few weeks back. Wilks had to admit that Clute's daring had generally paid off, given Wilks the kind of courage he hadn't had in a long time. Fine and dandy as long as he was able to overlook the night in Cheyenne when he'd found Clute standing over a man in the alley behind the saloon. Clute said that the man had cheated him at cards. But Wilks knew instantly that Clute was lying. Clute later admitted that he simply hadn't liked the man and had followed him out to the alley and had beaten and stomped him to death. When they'd finally gotten into the street and lamplight Wilks had seen that Clute's cuffs and boots were soaked with the man's blood. Pieces of brain glistened on the toe of one boot.

So now Clute had killed again. No reason to. Had been instructed several times *not* to. But as Clute was fond of saying, "I get real sick of takin' orders."

"You killed him! You killed him!" the driver screamed at Clute.

"You're part of this, mister," Clute said. "You better calm down."

"I was promised nobody'd be hurt—just like the first time."

All Wilks knew was that the driver's name was Newly Davis. He'd been in on the first one, too. He'd brought the stage to a halt and convinced this Hap Miller to hand over the money. Miller looked as if he might try something even after he'd been forced to give up his repeater but Newly Davis made sure he stayed calm. That was what Davis was being paid for. That was Wilks' understanding, anyway.

"Where's this big brave Fargo I keep hearin' so much about?" Clute said. He reached inside his shirt and brought out the pint of whiskey he usually carried with him. In the beginning Wilks had figured it was the whiskey that made Clute so crazy. But it didn't take him long to revise that opinion. Clute didn't need any help. He was plenty crazy without any whiskey. The liquor just put a polish on it.

But Davis was far from calming down. "You killed him—you know that? You killed Hap! You weren't supposed to kill nobody! Nobody!"

Wilks walked up to the coach and said, "Mr. Davis, you need to get hold of yourself. I'm sorry this happened. But it was an accident and now there isn't anything we can do about it."

"But he's dead! He's dead!"

"Please, Mr. Davis. We need to get this done and get out of here. Now hand down the box with all the money in it and we'll be on our way."

"Damned guy's like a little old lady," Clute said as he dismounted.

Wilks hoped Davis didn't hear it. Wilks also hoped that he could resist grabbing his own Colt and emptying it into Clute. The bastard had turned what was supposed to be a simple job into murder. That sheriff in Tall Rock was a wily son of a bitch. He'd already approached them to see what they were doing in his town. This murder would make things even more difficult.

"You have to do this for your sake as well as ours, Mr. Davis," Wilks said patiently. "A man has been killed. That means all three of us are involved in his death. Do you understand that, Mr. Davis? Maybe they wouldn't hang you but they'd sure put you away for a long time. Now I'm sure you've got a wife and family and that would be a hell of a thing if they put you away, wouldn't it?"

Davis' gaze narrowed. He began sniffling up the tears that stained his eyes and nostrils. He looked down at his dead friend and said, "I didn't kill him. Hap was my friend."

"But that won't make any difference to a jury, Mr. Davis. Now you get that box down here so we can get going. And then you head back to town."

"I'll have to tell his wife." Davis was back to sounding dazed.

"The box, Mr. Davis. Pick it up and hand it down to me." Then, to Clute: "How're you coming with Fargo?"

Clute laughed. "He's a big one."

With that Clute dragged the man from inside the coach. Fargo was unconscious, limp. Clute was as rough with him as he could be, slamming the back of Fargo's head against the step on the coach and then basically slamming him flat on the ground. "I bet there's a lot of people who'd like to see me kill this one right here and right now."

"Shut up, Clute," Wilks said, afraid his words would set Davis off again. He watched as Clute did his work, taking his pint bottle of rotgut and walking up and down the length of the big man's body, soaking every inch of it so that he would reek like a saloon.

As planned.

"I don't know what I'm gonna tell his wife," Davis said in that same dazed voice as he handed down the steel box with the fist-sized lock on it.

"You talk to the boss about this," Wilks said. "You don't talk to anybody else. You understand? He'll know what to do and what to say."

Clute came over. He talked as if Davis wasn't here. "You think maybe we should kill this one, too? I sure as hell don't want him walking around."

Clute's words had the effect of a strong slap across Davis' face. The mention of his own death brought him back to reality. "What's he talking about? Killing me? Is he talking about killing me?"

"He's just talking," Wilks said, glaring at Clute. He couldn't outdraw Clute but the way he was feeling now he wouldn't be against shooting him in the back if he had to. Do the human race a favor. "He talks all the time. It doesn't mean anything."

"You going to try and kill me?" Davis said to Clute. "I won't say anything. I promise."

For once Clute restrained himself. "That's all I needed

to hear, Mr. Davis. Now I'll load Fargo back into the coach and you head on back to town."

"What the hell'd you take him out of the coach for in the first place?" Wilks said.

"Not that it's any of your business but I was kind've hopin' he'd wake up once he was outside and go for his gun. Be nice to tell people I was the one who killed Skye Fargo."

"Oh, God," Davis said, "I can't believe what I got myself into."

"C'mon," Wilks said, disgusted and impatient now. "Let's get this finished up and get the hell out of here."

"I just can't believe it," Davis said. But he was talking to himself.

No other series packs this much heat!

THE TRAILSMAN

**Follow the trail of the gun-slinging heroes of
Penguin's Action Westerns at
penguin.com/actionwesterns**

"A writer in the tradition of Louis L'Amour
and Zane Grey!"
—*Huntsville Times*

National Bestselling Author
RALPH COMPTON

**Available wherever books are sold or at
penguin.com**